His stom
just then. Grace. Did she have any
idea he'd never gotten over
the first time he'd seen her?

Smitten about summed it up. Yeah, she was only fifteen at the time, and not exactly a fashion plate in ragged jeans and a faded T-shirt, her long, unruly hair rebelling against the thick braid she'd tried to force it into. But to a no-account kid like Ryan, sixteen and feeling his oats, she was Cameron Diaz, Taylor Swift, and Amy Adams all rolled into one.

Nothing beyond friendship ever came of their teenage crush, though. . . . Only later had he come to understand they were two needy people reaching out for the understanding and security they'd been starved for all their lives.

Drawing his thoughts back to the present, Ryan scrolled through his cell phone contacts for Grace's number. When she answered, he wedged a smile into his voice. "Hey, squirt."

MYRA JOHNSON

never thought she'd leave Texas, and she'll always be a Texan at heart, but sometimes you just have to go where the grandkids are. Nowadays she and her husband are enjoying the beauty of the Carolinas and living near three of their six grandchildren. Empty-nesters, the Johnsons share their home with two lovable dogs. Myra's first Heartsong Presents romance, *Autumn Rains,* won the 2005 RWA Golden Heart for Best Inspirational Romance Manuscript and was a 2010 ACFW Carol Award finalist. Find Myra on the web at www.myrajohnson.com and www.seekerville.net.

Books by Myra Johnson

HEARTSONG PRESENTS

A Horseman's Hope

Myra Johnson

Heartsong Presents

With gratitude to Pepper Basham for her insight into Asperger syndrome; Debby Giusti for fielding questions about army care teams; and Kerry Everett for her guidance regarding child custody law. Any errors are strictly my own. Also to Whitney McFrederick for "lending" me her little Pomeranian, Joy Bear, as a "supporting character"; Natasha Kern, the best agent ever; my husband and family for their unfailing support; and to my Lord and Savior, with whom all things are possible!

A note from the Author:

I love to hear from my readers! You may correspond with me by writing:

Myra Johnson
Author Relations
P.O. Box 9048
Buffalo, NY 14240-9048

ISBN-13: 978-0-373-48641-0

A HORSEMAN'S HOPE

Prologue

"I'm in trouble, Kip."

Ryan O'Keefe trusted no one more than Kip Lorimer, and he'd risk confiding in no one else. Especially after *this* life-changer of a foul-up.

"Ryan?" Kip's voice sounded scratchy over the weak cell phone connection. "Where are you?"

Ryan propped his boot heel on the rim of his pickup tire. His chest felt like he'd swallowed a baseball. "I'm at a gas station in Monroe. Can you meet me somewhere?"

Within the hour Kip joined him at an Arby's a few blocks away. Ryan had drained his cola long ago and now stabbed at the melting ice with a mangled straw.

Kip slid into the booth across from him, eyeing the attack on the ice. "If that varmint in there ain't dead yet, it's sure gonna be."

With a guilty shudder, Ryan pushed his drink cup aside. He shot his friend and mentor a nervous grin.

Kip laid his Stetson on the seat and then propped his forearms on the table, hands folded. "All right, I'm listenin'."

Ryan shifted his gaze sideways, glad the restaurant didn't have many customers this time of day. He lowered his voice anyway, clamping his teeth together. "It's my girlfriend. She's…pregnant."

"Aw, Ryan." Kip clawed stiff fingers through his short, sandy hair. He pulled in air through his nostrils. "You're a Christian. You know better."

Self-loathing seared Ryan's belly. His chin sank toward his chest. "It was just the one time, Kip, I promise. We… got carried away. *I* got carried away."

"You'll do right by her, of course."

"I will. I *want* to. But she won't marry me."

Kip shot him a worried glare. "She's not considering…"

"No. No!" Ryan's heart twisted at the very thought that Shana might get rid of the baby. "We've already talked about it. She's as antiabortion as I am."

"Then what are y'all planning to do?"

"Shana's gonna keep the baby." Ryan scraped a hand over tired eyes. "I'll help however she'll let me."

"Do her parents know?"

Ryan shook his head. "The Burches are hypocritical snobs. Shana won't have anything to do with them."

Kip stared out the window. "How're you figurin' to help raise a kid when you're supposed to be headed off to that Kentucky horseshoeing school?"

"By the time the baby comes, I'll be just a couple weeks from graduating. Then I'll move back here and…" The weight of it all forced the breath from Ryan's lungs. He could barely choke out his next words. "What am I gonna do, Kip? I'm not ready to have a kid. What if I'm—"

"Don't." Eyes blazing, Kip locked his fingers around Ryan's wrist. "Trust me, son. Just because you got bad parenting doesn't mean you're doomed to repeat those mistakes. You're stronger than that. Smarter, too. You've got the Lord on your side."

"You sure about that?" Ryan chewed his lip. "Like you said, I'm a Christian. I *know* sex outside of marriage is a sin, and now I'm reaping the consequences."

"Yep, consequences are guaranteed. But so is forgiveness. The Lord knows your heart. He'll see you through this—you, Shana, and that little baby, too."

Ryan's eyes misted. He squeezed out a weak smile for the quiet cowboy who, more than anyone else on earth, had helped him turn his sorry life around.

Then a tiny bubble of hope swelled beneath his breastbone. *Dear Jesus, I'm gonna be a father!*

Chapter 1

I'm a father!

Four years now and Ryan still felt like pinching himself every time he laid eyes on his precious little girl. With chocolate-brown hair and eyes the color of Carolina pines, Christina Hope O'Keefe could dazzle the socks off a stone-cold statue.

"Christina, honey, grab your backpack. We gotta go."

Ignoring him, Christina skewed her mouth to the left and concentrated even harder on the horse drawing she'd been working on instead of finishing a bowl of frosted wheat squares that grew soggier by the minute.

Ryan hauled in a breath and prayed for an extra dose of patience, something he'd needed plenty of since his little girl had been diagnosed with Asperger syndrome a few months before her fourth birthday.

Which was about the time Shana had decided she couldn't handle being a mom anymore.

"That's a fine horse, sweetie." Slipping into his denim jacket, Ryan peered over Christina's shoulder at a detailed sketch that would have been considered exceptional for a kid twice her age. Gently he slid the pencil from between her fingers. Would he ever remember the direct approach worked better for Aspies? "Christina, it's work time, not drawing time. Put your tablet and pencils in your backpack."

"This is a mare. She has thirty-six teeth." Christina scooted off the chair.

"Yep, and we've got thirty-six minutes to get over to Mr. Gardner's place so I can shoe Velvet." Ryan held his daughter's backpack open while she shoved her sketchbook inside. "Now get your jacket so we can go, kiddo."

"Velvet is a Friesian mare." Christina worked one arm and then the other into a pink fleece hoodie. "Friesians are good carriage horses."

"Indeed they are." Tucking his daughter's hand into his own, Ryan opened the back door of his rented two-bedroom bungalow, where he'd settled in Kingsley, North Carolina.

The spring-fresh morning carried the scent of dewy grass and damp earth. A little brown bird poked its beak at the cake of suet hanging from a low tree branch.

Christina pointed. "There's our Carolina wren. Its eggs should be hatching very soon." A few days ago Ryan had spoken those very same words, cadence and all, when he'd shown her the tiny domed nest the wrens had built in the ivy planter outside the kitchen window.

"Maybe we'll get to watch. That would be fun, huh?" Ryan guided his daughter down the porch steps. He did his best to make sure Christina had every opportunity to stretch and grow, to challenge that bright little mind. So she wasn't exactly like other kids. So she had some social development issues. Like he didn't? At least his child wasn't growing up with an alcoholic father and a mother who couldn't cope.

Okay, maybe Shana wasn't exactly *coping* either, begging him to take Christina and then requesting transfer from Army Reserves to active duty. But Ryan could hardly blame her for panicking. The Asperger diagnosis, though on the milder end of the autism scale, had knocked them both for a loop.

Halfway to the driveway, Christina jerked on Ryan's hand. "Daddy, we should go back in the house."

"No, honey. I told you; we're going to see Mr. Gardner's mare." Ryan tried to urge his daughter toward the pickup, but she'd planted her pink sneakers firmly into their scraggly lawn.

She shook her head. "I need to go in the house."

Now what? Ryan was still learning the ins and outs of parenting an Asperger child. Was she just being stubborn, or—

Without warning, Christina bent forward and upchucked what little breakfast she'd eaten all over the toes of Ryan's boots.

"Aw, honey!" He scooped her into his arms and marched to the house. After setting her down on the porch, he tried not to inhale while hurriedly shucking his befouled boots. "Why didn't you tell me you felt sick?"

She shifted her mouth sideways, her fingers flicking rapidly. "I can't talk about it."

"Of course you can. You can talk to me about anything." Ryan made sure his hand was clean before digging his keys from his pocket.

"But you told me not to say the throw-up word."

"I did?" Racking his brain for when he could possibly have imparted this bit of parental guidance, Ryan unlocked the door and ushered his daughter inside.

By the time they reached the bathroom, he'd remembered. Several weeks ago they'd been on a farrier call at Cross Roads Farm. Nathan Cross and his wife, Filipa, were watching Ryan trim Shadow's hooves, when suddenly Filipa thrust a hand over her mouth and bolted from the barn. Grinning sheepishly, Nathan had mumbled something about morning sickness, and of course Christina wanted to know what that meant.

Now, as he brushed a wet washcloth across Christina's face, she looked up at him with a worried frown. "Velvet needs her shoes in thirty-six minutes."

"We can't give Velvet her shoes if you're sick, honey."

"But Velvet needs her shoes!" Christina's hands flapped at her sides, a habit she'd developed to help calm herself. "Poor Velvet."

Ryan's heart melted. "Velvet will be okay. I'll call Mr. Gardner and tell him we'll come another day. I'm more worried about you right now." He pressed the back of his hand against Christina's forehead then her cheeks. Definitely warm. Why hadn't he noticed earlier? And she always ate all her breakfast. The fact that she hadn't this morning should have clued him in.

He hadn't been a dad long enough to second-guess his kid's health. Better head to the clinic and have her checked out. He led Christina to the kitchen, where he found a small plastic pail under the sink and then grabbed a wad of paper towels, explaining to her the reason for each item as they went. Over the past few months he'd learned, often the hard way, that the best way to keep Christina calm was to be very clear and direct.

He trotted to his closet for a clean pair of boots, crow-hopped to the kitchen while working his feet into them, and then headed out the door again with Christina.

Reaching his red extended-cab pickup, Ryan yanked

open the rear door and buckled Christina into her booster seat. Without taking time to unhitch his mobile farrier trailer, he backed down the gravel driveway and turned toward downtown Kingsley. Ten minutes later he pulled the rig to the far edge of the parking area beside Kingsley Community Medical Clinic.

At least Christina hadn't thrown up again, which he hoped was a good sign. Ryan stuffed the paper towels into his jacket pocket just in case before hefting Christina onto his hip. His heart shivered when she snuggled her head against his shoulder.

Thank goodness he found Grace Lorimer behind the reception counter this morning. Unlike her counterpart, a seasoned mother of four, Grace wouldn't give him grief about being a neurotic, overprotective dad.

Not to mention Grace had owned a big chunk of Ryan's heart for years now. Not that she had any clue, of course. But if circumstances had been different—if *they'd* been different—

He had to keep reminding himself that if he'd never met Shana, they wouldn't have Christina, and the precious little girl cuddled in his arms meant more to him than anything or anyone.

Caressing his daughter's downy-soft hair, Ryan returned his thoughts to the present and sidled up to the counter. "Hey, squirt."

Grace snapped her head up and grinned. "Hey, scuzzy." Then she glanced at Christina, and her hazel eyes turned serious. "Uh-oh, somebody must not feel very good."

"She threw up on my boots. I think she has a fever."

"Daddy..." Christina pinched his shoulder. "You said the throw-up word."

"It's okay, bunny. Grace is a trained professional. We

can use that word with her." Ryan braced his elbow on the counter. "Any chance you can work us in?"

Grace twisted her strawberry-blond ponytail while she flipped through screens on her computer monitor. "Dr. Grundmann has an opening. She's seen Christina before, hasn't she?"

"Yeah, when we came in for a checkup and flu shots last fall." Ryan gnawed his lip. "She couldn't be getting the flu this late, could she?"

"Not likely." Grace typed something into her computer then smiled up at him. "It'll be twenty minutes or so. Have a seat and the nurse will call you."

"Thanks, squirt."

Grace winked. "No prob, scuzzy."

Ryan chuckled to himself. They'd called each other by those "endearments" for ages, almost since their friendship began out at Cross Roads Farm. As a teenager Ryan had been a client at the therapeutic riding center, busing out to the farm with the other messed-up kids from his group home. The little sister of Kip Lorimer, the barn manager, Grace had been a pretty messed-up kid herself when Ryan first met her.

They'd both come a long, long way since then. Ryan had earned a vocational degree in equine management, graduated from farrier school, and now operated a lucrative horseshoeing business. Grace was working toward an exercise science degree at UNC Charlotte with plans to become an occupational therapist. In the meantime, she worked part-time at the clinic and also taught or assisted with the Cross Roads Farm riding classes.

With Christina drowsing against his chest, Ryan made a quick call to Mr. Gardner then picked up a dog-eared *Prevention* magazine and flipped through the pages. When he came to a full-color advertisement featuring a lithe brunette, Christina popped her head up and stated, "Look, there's Mommy."

Ryan's stomach knotted. "No, honey. It just looks like Mommy. Mommy is in Afghanistan, remember?"

Christina laid her head back on Ryan's shoulder. "Buzkashi is the national sport of Afghanistan," she said, repeating something Ryan had read to her from a book about horses. "It requires a high degree of horsemanship."

"That's right." Ryan gently stilled his daughter's fluttering hands, the only outward sign of her concern. Christina may not process or express emotions in the same way other children do, but in her own way she missed her mom.

As for Ryan's emotions, he struggled daily. He hated that Christina's mother was clear across the globe, hated the idea of Shana putting her life at risk every day. Why couldn't she have married him five years ago when he'd asked her to? They could have given their daughter the kind of family he'd hoped she'd have. Even more, they could have been there for each other.

"Yes, Mrs. Hodges, we did get that prescription called in. Check with your pharmacy in about an hour, okay?" With a polite good-bye, Grace pushed the disconnect button on her telephone headset. Returning her attention to a mound of insurance forms, she glanced across the rapidly filling waiting room. Good thing all three staff doctors were in today. Must be an epidemic of stomach bugs going around.

When her gaze landed on Ryan O'Keefe, her heart did a tiny flip. All these years later she still hadn't gotten over her teenage crush. The brooding "bad boy" from the group home—hence the nickname *scuzzy*—had always held a certain allure, despite the fact that by the time Grace met Ryan, he was already changing his life for the better.

Yes, Grace's big brother, Kip, definitely had that effect

on people. And horses. And dogs. Grace would never forget the day she met her soft-spoken older brother for the very first time—and she'd never forgive their mother for keeping Kip a secret as long as she had.

In fact, there was quite a bit she'd never forgive her mother for. Didn't matter how hard the woman tried to ditch her addictions. Didn't matter how many promises she made. Some things about the woman never changed. Grace had seen her mother fail too many times in too many ways, and she wasn't about to risk getting disappointed again.

By her mom, or anyone else.

"Who's next?" Ivy Sumner, Dr. Grundmann's nurse, stepped up beside Grace and lifted the next file from the appointment slot. "Oh, it's Christina. Such a sweet thing."

"Looks like she might have that stomach virus everyone's been calling in with." Grace peered into the waiting area and saw that Christina had fallen asleep against Ryan's chest. He rested his cheek atop the little girl's head as he browsed a magazine.

Such a good dad. Devoted, attentive, involved. And he did it all by himself. Shana Burch might be serving her country, but there was more behind her choice than just that. How she could have deserted both Ryan and the daughter they shared just blew Grace's mind.

Ivy opened the outer door and softly called Christina's name. Ryan looked up with a start before gently shifting his weight so he could stand without disturbing the sleeping child more than necessary. Christina sagged in his arms like a life-size puppet whose strings had been snipped, her fuzzy pink hoodie drooping off one shoulder.

Ryan caught Grace's eye on his way through and mouthed a thank-you. Grace wished she could soothe away the worry lines around his eyes and remind him how resilient kids are.

The phone rang again, and Grace shifted back into receptionist mode. "Kingsley Community Medical Clinic."

"Hey, kiddo."

"Kip?" Her brother rarely bothered her at work. Grace swiveled away from the desk. "What's up?"

"Can you put one of the nurses on? We, uh…we got problems here."

The tension in Kip's voice sent warning signals through Grace's limbs. "Are you hurt?"

"Not me. It's Sheridan. She's…" He gulped, sniffed, cleared his throat.

"Oh, Kip." Grace bit the inside of her lip. "Let me find someone. Hold on." With Kip's line on hold, she buzzed the nurses' intercom.

Seconds later Ivy picked up, and it was all Grace could do to keep from listening in as Ivy took Kip's call.

Dear God, please don't let it be another miscarriage. They've wanted a baby for so long!

Nobody on the planet deserved to be parents more than Kip and Sheridan. Grace hated to think where she'd be today if Kip and the Crosses hadn't taken her in when Mom dumped her off with them before checking herself into a rehab center.

For all the good rehab had done. Six months later Mom was drinking again and shacking up with yet another loser. Grace had lost count of how many times her mother had cycled in and out of bad relationships with both booze and men.

As soon as Grace saw the light on her phone blink out, she ripped off the headset and marched down the hall to the nurses' station. She found Ivy jotting notes in a chart. "What did Kip say? How's Sheridan?"

Frowning, Ivy gave her head a sad shake, causing tortoiseshell glasses to slip down her nose. "It doesn't sound good. They should see Sheridan's OB/GYN as soon as possible."

Which meant a half-hour drive to a Charlotte suburb. Definitely one of the disadvantages of small-town living.

Dr. Gloria Grundmann exited one of the exam rooms and crossed the corridor into the nurses' area. She handed Ivy a manila folder and pointed to a yellow sticky note on top. "I think a rep left us some samples of this drug last week. Would you give Ryan a week's worth of the pediatric dose? Then they're free to go."

"On it, Doc." Ivy took the folder. "Oh, and you might want to follow up on this one." She handed the doctor Sheridan Lorimer's chart.

Giving Ivy's notes a cursory glance, Dr. Grundmann drew air between her teeth. She patted Grace's arm. "Tell Sheridan and your brother how sorry I am. Remind them they've got my cell number if the bleeding worsens or if there's anything else I can do."

Having a doctor who knew you personally and cared enough to give out her private number? Definitely one of the pluses of small-town living.

A few minutes after Grace returned to the front, Ryan and Christina appeared at the checkout window. Grace perused the superbill. "Same insurance info, so your copay is ten dollars."

"Got it right here." Ryan set Christina on the narrow counter while he dug in his back pocket for his wallet.

As Grace made a notation on the bill, the pen slipped from her fingers and skittered to the floor. She yanked another pen from the round metal holder and flipped the cap off with her thumb, only to send the cap flying across the desk. She muttered a mild expletive.

Ryan gave a bemused chuckle. "Settle down, squirt. It's just a pen."

"Sorry, I..." Grace flattened her palms atop the paperwork strewn across the work space. "Why is it the people who should never be parents are the ones who have kids, and the people who'd make the best parents in the world never get the chance?"

Stiffening, Ryan slid a ten-dollar bill across the counter. He stuffed a small white bag of prescription samples into his jacket pocket and then balanced Christina on the opposite hip. "If I could have my receipt..."

"Right." Grace finished with the superbill, entered the data into the O'Keefes' computer record, and then waited for the printer to spit out Ryan's receipt.

It wasn't until she watched him march out the door without so much as a backward glance or his usual "See ya, squirt," that she realized how cruel her words had sounded.

I didn't mean you, Ryan. Please forgive me, I didn't mean you!

Chapter 2

"Hi, Ryan. How's Christina? Can I talk to her?" Shana's grainy image filled Ryan's laptop screen. She wore army fatigues, and a billed cap hid most of her close-cropped mahogany curls. Behind her, other soldiers meandered about the rec room of the unit's Afghanistan headquarters.

Ryan set the computer on the coffee table then scooted to the sofa's edge, fingers laced between his knees. "Sorry, she's still asleep. She came down with a tummy bug a couple of days ago."

Shana frowned. "Is she okay?"

"Nothing a day or two of lemon-lime soda and saltines won't cure. The worst part was putting up with her tantrum when she found out she'd miss her riding therapy class."

"You took her to the doctor, of course?" Shana's face moved closer to the lens.

"First thing. She's fine, I promise." Ryan stifled a huff. Shana had a right to be concerned about their daughter, but give him some credit, okay? Who was the one cleaning throw-up off his boots? Who got up in the middle of the night when Christina's tummy hurt so bad she couldn't sleep? Who took two days off work to stay home with her?

Not that he'd trade a minute of it. And not that he begrudged Shana's service to her country. But she was Christina's mom, for crying out loud! What was she doing half a world away—intentionally avoiding their daughter's challenges—when they needed her right here?

"Ryan...you know I appreciate all you're doing for Christina." The apologetic tone and guilty slant of her mouth told Ryan she was about to sign off. "Tell her I called, okay?"

"Yeah. I'll...give her your love." Even though Shana hadn't asked him to. She never used the word *love*. Not to Ryan, even when they were so enamored with each other that they managed to make a baby together. And never once to Christina, her own flesh and blood.

Ryan wondered if Shana knew how to love anyone.

The video call ended, and Ryan sank into the sofa cushions with a groan. He supposed he should be grateful Shana made a point of checking in with them every week. In her own way she cared about Christina, but Ryan blamed Shana's materialistic parents for failing as examples of what real parental love should be.

Grace's words from two days ago rushed back: *"Why is it the people who should never be parents are the ones who have kids?"* Shana's folks sure fit that bill.

But if they hadn't had Shana, he'd never have met her. Which meant he wouldn't have Christina—exactly where his circular reasoning always ended up.

And he loved that little girl like life itself.

He scraped his palms down his face. *The people who should never be parents...* He wanted to believe Grace's comment hadn't been directed at him. He wanted to believe he was a good father. Because God knew he tried his best.

Dear Lord, give me strength, give me wisdom.

With a sigh he pushed up from the sofa. The clock on the cable box read 7:52. He'd give the sleepyhead a little more rack time, but then he'd have to wake her so they could head out on his farrier calls.

An hour later, with Christina buckled into her car seat and a backpack filled with snacks, colored pencils, a sketchbook, and three of her favorite illustrated horse books tucked next to her, Ryan backed the pickup and farrier trailer down the driveway.

"How many horses will we see today, Daddy?"

"Bunches and bunches, sugarplum." Ryan grinned at his daughter through the rearview mirror. "There's Mr. Tatum's quarter horse with the big white star…"

"Darby. He's seven years old and stands fifteen hands tall. Darby had colic on November twelfth. Mr. Tatum had to call the vet."

"Right." Ryan chuckled to himself. That was four months ago. How did the kid remember this stuff? Half the time Ryan couldn't even remember his own birthday.

"Who else, Daddy? Because if I haven't drawn their picture yet, I need to today."

Ryan made the next turn and then slid his gaze to the mirror. "Why today?"

"Because you said you wouldn't buy me a new sketchbook until I use this one up." Christina quirked her lips and stared out the side window. "And I need one with bigger pages."

Great. When would Ryan ever learn that Christina took everything literally? "I meant you should keep using the sketchbook you have until I can get to the arts-and-crafts store to buy you a new one."

"Oh." Christina puffed air between her lips. Her tiny brow wrinkled in consternation, as if she didn't understand why her own father couldn't make sense.

Again she asked for a complete rundown on the horses they'd be visiting. By the time Ryan finished naming them all and Christina had interjected her not-to-be-forgotten facts, they arrived at the Tatum place just across the state line outside Lancaster, South Carolina. While Ryan trimmed Darby's hooves, Christina sat in the pickup cab and worked on her horse drawings.

Mr. Tatum propped his foot on an upturned feed bucket. "That little sweetheart of yours gets cuter every time I see her. Heard from her mother lately?"

"Just this morning." Ryan steadied Darby's left hind leg while he used the nippers to trim the hoof. He didn't particularly care to be reminded of Shana's call and realized he'd conveniently forgotten to mention it to Christina. He'd be sure to tell her later, though. She needed to know her mom cared.

Scratch that. It was really Ryan who needed to know Shana cared. Despite her refusal to marry him and make a family for their daughter together, he couldn't help loving her. Over time he'd come to realize they'd never truly been *in love*—infatuation better described what they'd had—but he still cared deeply for the mother of his child.

Mr. Tatum ambled over and handed Ryan the rasp. "Well, God willing, they'll settle that Afghanistan business one o' these days and Christina's mommy can come home. I know you must miss her somethin' awful."

"Yeah. We do." But not in the way Mr. Tatum suggested. What Ryan regretted more than anything was not being able to give Christina the loving two-parent home he'd never had.

"Daddy," Christina called through the open pickup window, "your phone is ringing."

"Can you read the caller ID?"

"C-R-O-S-S-R-O-A—"

"Cross Roads Farm. Answer it, sweetie." Ryan finished filing down the hoof and then reattached the shoe. Releasing Darby's foot to the ground, Ryan checked the horse's stance. "Looks good. Be right back," he told Mr. Tatum.

Ryan strode over to the pickup and leaned in the window. "What'd they say?"

"Lady threw a shoe. Mr. Kip said to come over as soon as it's convenient."

A smile teased Ryan's lips. He doubted Christina even knew what *convenient* meant. Her speaking vocabulary far outpaced her comprehension. "Thanks, honey. We'll catch him on the way home this afternoon."

"But he's not running."

"Running?"

"You said we had to catch him."

Ryan gave himself a mental head slap. Nope, he'd never learn.

By four o'clock he'd finished his scheduled appointments and was headed back toward Kingsley. While stopped at the gas station to fill up, he phoned Kip. "Hey, just letting you know I'll be there in about twenty minutes."

"Oh, uh, thanks. We've got a class going on, but Lady will be in her stall."

Something in Kip's tone made Ryan uneasy. "Everything okay?"

When Kip didn't respond right away, Ryan wondered if the call had dropped. Finally Kip muttered a terse, "Yeah. Fine. See you in a bit."

Kip Lorimer might be a man of few words, but Ryan had known him long enough to sense when something wasn't right. He'd like to believe Kip was merely preoccupied with farm business, but his gut told him otherwise.

Sliding into the driver's seat, he swiveled to check on Christina. "Still buckled in, sugarplum?"

She puckered her lips. "Daddy, my name is Christina. You keep forgetting."

"No, I don't." Ryan buckled his own seat belt and then started the engine. He grinned into the rearview mirror. "I like calling you 'sugarplum.' And 'honeybunch.' And 'punkin.' And just all sorts of sweet names, because you're so sweet."

As he turned onto the country road that led to Cross Roads Farm, Ryan sent up another prayer of thanksgiving to his heavenly Father for sending Christina into his life. This little girl was the absolute best thing that had ever happened to him, and anyone who referred to Asperger's as a "disorder" ought to have *their* head examined.

Grace peeked into the master bedroom, where Sheridan sat propped up in bed beneath a light blanket. The sight of her sister-in-law's hollow cheeks and vacant expression squeezed Grace's heart. "Can I get you anything, Sher?"

As if returning from a dark, faraway place, Sheridan slowly turned her head. Her chest rose and fell in a long, whispery sigh. "No... . Well, maybe some tea."

"Be right back." Starting downstairs, Grace sniffed back a tear. She hated seeing the grief in Sheridan's eyes, hated knowing Kip was suffering just as much. They wanted kids so badly! *Why, God?*

Her thoughts returned to her insensitive remark to Ryan the other day, and guilt welled once more. She hoped to get the chance to apologize when he came to reshoe Lady.

In the kitchen she started the electric teakettle and then opened a packet of hibiscus tea. As she placed the tea bag in a ceramic mug, the rumble of tires over gravel announced someone's arrival. She glanced out the kitchen window to see Ryan's pickup come to a stop in front of the barn. Her breath hitched. Nerves? Embarrassment?

For heaven's sake, how long had they known each other? At least six or seven years now. Long enough to get past the remnants of a hopeless teenage crush and start relating like mature adults.

Adults who continued to call each other silly names like *squirt* and *scuzzy*.

Grace let a smile tickle her lips. Ryan was a good friend, and she truly regretted hurting him. He'd be busy with Lady for a while, but she'd catch him before he finished. She'd apologize and explain how worried and upset she'd been after Kip's phone call to the clinic, and then everything would be fine.

Fine, if she didn't count the fact that she'd never quite gotten over being jealous of Shana.

The teakettle clicked off, and Grace filled the mug. She set it on a small tray along with a napkin, spoon, and saucer then carried the tray upstairs. Returning to Sheridan's room, Grace stepped around Xena, the big black Great Dane who was never far from Sheridan's side—even more so since old Beau, the Crosses' chocolate Lab, had passed away last year.

"Here you go, Sher. It's hibiscus, your favorite. Are you sure you don't want something to eat? Maybe some toast and jam?"

Sheridan adjusted her pillows and motioned for Grace to set the tray on the nightstand, casting her a sad-eyed smile. "Thanks, but…I'm just…not hungry."

Plopping onto the edge of the bed, Grace clutched her sister-in-law's hand. "Honey, you've got to keep your strength up so your body can heal."

Sheridan's face contorted. Her words came out in a

strained whisper. "But my heart is *never* going to heal. I can't keep doing this, Grace. I can't go through this again. *Ever.*"

"I know you feel that way now, but you can't give up hope. Give it time, Sher. There has to be an answer."

"God's already given us our answer." Glancing away, Sheridan set her mouth in a firm line. "How could He say it any more clearly?"

Realizing nothing she could say would make a difference, Grace gave Sheridan's hand a final squeeze and then stood. She forced down the lump in her throat. "Don't let your tea get cold. I'll check on you later."

"Grace…?"

She halted in the doorway. "What is it, Sher?"

"I'm glad you're here."

The four o'clock therapeutic riding class was well under way by the time Grace started out to the barn. Sheridan usually led this class of five kids with varying levels of cognitive disabilities, but today Kassie Kvello, one of the other instructors, had stepped in.

Pausing to watch the class, Grace admired Kassie's natural way of encouraging the riders' body control, verbal skills, and problem-solving abilities. Kassie had mentored Grace through instructor training and certification, and though Grace now taught two Saturday riding skills classes, she longed to have the knowledge and ability to work effectively with physically disabled riders. Just another year or so and she'd have enough hours for her exercise science undergraduate degree, and then she could finally start on her master's in occupational therapy.

If she could continue balancing schoolwork with part-time employment—the only way she'd ever be able to afford her education.

With a sigh, she continued on to the barn. Inside, she found Lady in the cross-ties and Sheridan's brother, Nathan, keeping the horse quiet while Ryan worked on her right front hoof.

Nathan looked up at Grace's approach. "Hey, kiddo. How's my big sis doing?"

"Resting. Wish there were more I could do." Grace patted Nathan's shoulder on her way around to Ryan's side of the horse.

Ryan cocked his head to smile at Grace as he ran the rasp across Lady's hoof. "Hey, squirt."

Grace swallowed. "Ryan, about what I said the other day..."

"No need to explain. Soon as Nathan told me what happened, I realized you were just upset." He nodded toward his pickup. "Go say hi to Christina. She's got some new pictures to show you."

"Is she feeling better? All over her tummy bug?"

"All better." Ryan laid aside the rasp then reached for a shiny steel horseshoe and measured it against Lady's hoof. His sweat-glazed biceps flexed beneath the sleeves of a blue T-shirt.

Grace stepped back, hugging herself against an unexpected quiver in her belly. This was *Ryan*, for heaven's sake. Her friend. Period. Not to mention she was pretty sure Ryan still carried a torch for Shana. They did share a child together, after all. Besides, Grace had sworn off romance years ago, thanks to her mother's shining example.

With a stiff smile, she marched over to the pickup and peeked in the passenger-side window. "Hi, Christina. Your daddy said you have some new drawings. Can I see?"

Cheeks dimpled in concentration, Christina added a few more pencil strokes to an amazing sketch of a cantering horse. "The canter is a three-beat gait. See how all four feet are off the ground at the same time?"

"I see that." Grace could only shake her head in awe. This kid was becoming a walking, talking equine encyclopedia. Not to mention a gifted artist. Grace wished she'd known even half as much about horses at Christina's age.

"Pretty amazing, huh?" Ryan had come up beside her. He reached into the pickup bed for a denim jacket and tattered blue Carolina Panthers ball cap. "Say, don't you usually have a UNC class on Thursday afternoon?"

"I do. But I wanted to be here for Sheridan." Tucking her hands into her jeans pockets, Grace glanced toward the main house.

"Gotta be tough," Ryan muttered. He slipped into his jacket and cap on his way to the farrier trailer. "Even harder knowing Nathan and Filipa have a little one on the way."

Grace watched as Ryan stowed his tools and then latched the doors. "I know Sheridan and Kip are happy for them, but you're right. I've seen the envy in Sheridan's eyes whenever Fil talks about feeling the baby move or shows off something cute she picked up at the baby store."

A volunteer horse leader rounded the pickup, returning Gem to the barn. "Class must be over," Grace said. "I should see if Kip needs help shutting things down."

"Why don't you let me?" Ryan caught her arm. "That is, if you wouldn't mind keeping an eye on Christina for a few minutes. I'd like to talk to Kip, tell him how sorry I am."

"Just don't make a big deal out of it, okay? You know Kip." Grace shrugged. "A cowboy's got to keep a stiff upper lip."

Chapter 3

"I don't know if spending the night is such a good idea, Mrs. Burch." Ryan pinched his cell phone between his ear and shoulder as he set another supper plate in the dishwasher. "Christina's used to a certain routine, and I don't like messing with it."

"I wish you wouldn't be so stubborn about these visits." The woman's haughty tone grated on Ryan's nerves. "We're Christina's grandparents. We have a right to spend time with her."

"Well, I'm her father, and I need to do what I think is best."

A pause. "For her…or for you?"

He slammed the dishwasher door shut, glad he'd already tucked Christina into bed before Shana's mother phoned. "I resent that, Mrs. Burch. I've bent over backward to accommodate any reasonable request for a visit."

The woman harrumphed. "Shana should never have agreed to shared custody with you."

"Well, she might not have, if her parents hadn't practically disowned her the minute they found out she was pregnant."

That shut her up. For a moment, anyway. "We certainly didn't raise our daughter to turn out so headstrong and rebellious."

Actually, I think it was self-defense. Ryan switched off the kitchen light on his way to the living room. He sank onto the sofa and propped his feet on the coffee table. "Look, I don't want to argue with you. Don't mean to cause problems either. But last time I let Christina stay over, I had to drive all the way to Shelby in the middle of the night because she wouldn't stop screaming. It was almost a week before I got her back into a regular sleep schedule."

"That…was unfortunate. We know better now." Mrs. Burch huffed a sigh. "And doesn't it seem foolish for either of us to make that three-hour round-trip for only a short visit?"

"I'm happy to bring her over Sunday afternoon." *Not.* He'd rather walk barefoot over hot coals than spend five minutes with the Burches. But family was important, and he wanted Christina to know her grandparents. She'd already had a positive effect on Ryan's mother, who, surprisingly, was becoming a pretty good grandma. Was it too much to hope Christina might also teach the Burches a thing or two about love?

"Clearly, reasoning with you is an exercise in futility. In that case, we shall plan to see you and Christina on Sunday afternoon—and the earlier, the better." The line went dead.

Groaning, Ryan tossed his phone to the other end of the sofa. He supposed he should be thankful the Burches were only Christina's grandparents and not also his in-laws. At least Shana had agreed from the start that she and Ryan would share custody of Christina, which made their daughter's transition much easier after Shana's deployment.

Not that Ryan had been prepared for full-time fatherhood. Every day was a learning experience. Ryan had weighed the pros and cons of leaving Christina in the daycare center where Shana had been taking her, but once they found out about the Asperger's, he didn't like the idea of entrusting his little girl into the care of people with little or no understanding of the syndrome. No matter how good they were with "normal" kids or how sterling their reputation, nobody could cherish Christina or respond to her needs better than her very own daddy.

And so Ryan dived headfirst into the parenting thing. He started taking Christina everywhere with him, including his farrier calls. Always content to sit in the pickup or a client's kitchen or barn office with her sketch pad, horse books, and a backpack full of snacks, she never caused him a lick of trouble. His clients thought she was adorable, not to mention the smartest thing since sliced bread.

Sure, the day would eventually come when he'd have to find the right school for her, but for now he was happy just spending time with his special little girl. Every dad should be so lucky.

The thought brought Kip and Sheridan's loss to mind, and Ryan's stomach churned. Kip had put up a brave front yesterday, but Ryan could see the heartbreak behind the cowboy's eyes. Maybe he should call and let his best friend know he was praying for them.

But as he fished his phone from a crack between the sofa cushions, second thoughts plagued him. Rather than risk disturbing Kip or Sheridan, maybe he should call Grace instead.

His stomach did another weird twist just then. *Grace.*

Did she have any idea he'd never gotten over the first time he'd seen her? *Smitten* about summed it up. Yeah, she was only fifteen at the time, and not exactly a fashion plate in ragged jeans and a faded T-shirt, her long, unruly hair rebelling against the thick braid she'd tried to force it into. But to a no-account kid like Ryan, sixteen and feeling his oats, she was Cameron Diaz, Taylor Swift, and Amy Adams all rolled into one.

Nothing beyond friendship ever came of their teenage crush, though. Ryan had been too busy staying out of trouble and trying to get his act together. Grace had adjustments of her own to deal with, what with her mom hauling her clear across the country to sign guardianship over to a brother Grace hadn't even known about before arriving in Kingsley.

Then in junior college Ryan had met Shana, a girl with a mind of her own and no shortage of attitude. She had intrigued him, challenged him, elicited manly feelings in him he'd mistaken for love. Only later had he come to understand they were two needy people reaching out for the understanding and security they'd been starved for all their lives.

Drawing his thoughts back to the present, Ryan scrolled through his cell phone contacts for Grace's number. When she answered, he wedged a smile into his voice. "Hey, squirt."

"Hey, scuzzy." Grace couldn't suppress a grin as she carried a cup of chamomile tea over to the aging plaid sofa. It had been a long day, and she was ready to put her feet up for a while.

"I wondered how Kip and Sheridan are doing. They've been on my mind all day." Ryan's tone sounded different somehow, more subdued than usual.

"They'll get through this." At least Grace hoped so. "I sat with Sheridan most of the day and made supper for her and Kip. Just got back from cleaning up the kitchen." She gazed through the front windows of the caretaker's cottage and watched the lights in the main house flicker out. Kip and Sheridan must be even more exhausted than Grace.

Ryan's sigh whispered through the phone connection. "Wish there were something I could do. This is...so unfair."

Grace set her mug of tea on an end table. "Ryan, are *you* okay?"

"Me? Yeah, sure." He snorted. "Why wouldn't I be?"

"Well, because you don't sound like yourself. If you're worried about Kip and Sheridan—"

"You bet I am. It kills me to see them hurting like this."

Grace sensed an unspoken *but* at the end of Ryan's statement. She curled her bare feet under her and stretched one arm along the back of the sofa. "Is this about Christina? Because if you're having any doubts whatsoever about what a great dad you are, then let me set you straight right now."

Ryan groaned. "I didn't call to talk about *my* problems."

"Then you admit you have problems." Grace pictured the little-boy look in Ryan's eyes, the one he always tried so hard to disguise behind a tough exterior. "What is it, Ry? Talk to me."

"It's nothing. Really." That macho I-don't-need-anyone tone from his teen years had crept into his voice.

Grace rolled her eyes. *Men.* "Don't make me come over there and force it out of you."

Silence. Then, "Would you? Come over, I mean."

Her breath caught. "You're serious?"

"Hey, crazy idea. Forget it." Ryan's fake laugh was totally unconvincing.

"No, let's *not* forget it. I can be there in twenty minutes."

She might be utterly drained, both physically and emotionally, but no way she'd ignore a troubled friend's plea.

Tuning out his continued protests, Grace cut him off with a terse, "Cool it, O'Keefe. I'm coming whether you like it or not." Five minutes later she was on the road.

Arriving at Ryan's house, she parked behind his farrier trailer then marched across the backyard and up the porch steps. Ryan pulled the door open before she could tap on the glass.

"You didn't have to drive all the way over here," he said, eyes lowered and one hand jammed into his jeans pocket.

"You obviously needed to talk." Grace sidled into the kitchen, noting two clean but faded horse-print place mats on the small dinette. A faint aroma of grilled chicken lingered. As a single dad who not only ran a successful farrier business but also cleaned and cooked, Ryan had no business dabbling in self-doubt.

Whereas self-doubt pretty much ruled Grace's life.

But she hadn't come here to wallow in her own issues. She crossed to the living room and plopped into a green slip-covered chair then put on a half-teasing attitude. "I mean it, scuzzy. I'm tired and in no mood for arm twisting. So spill your guts so I can get on with the 'tea and sympathy' thing and go home to bed."

"Well, since you put it like that…" Ryan snickered as he collapsed onto the sofa. Then, with a groan, he ground his eye sockets with the heels of his hands. "Okay, okay. It's Shana's folks. They keep pressuring me to give them more time with Christina. But these visits never turn out well, and anything longer than a couple of hours with the Burches totally upsets Christina's equilibrium."

Grace pursed her lips. "Can't you just say no?"

"How can I deny Christina's grandparents?" A frustrated

growl worked its way up through Ryan's chest. "I promised I'd take her over again on Sunday."

"I'm sorry, Ryan. I can't even imagine how hard this is for you." Grace sat forward and reached for his hand. The soft flesh of his palm, rimmed by a row of stubborn calluses, felt warm and clean. An idea popped into her head. "What if I went along with you? I could keep you company while Christina visits the Burches."

"I couldn't ask you to do that." He ran his thumb across the back of her hand in a way that made her shiver. "Anyway, wouldn't you rather be around in case Sheridan needs you?"

"She and Kip could use some alone time this weekend. It'll be fine." Still feeling Ryan's touch, she pulled her hand into her lap and tried to recapture some perspective. Teenage crushes were just that—childish and self-limiting. Even if Ryan weren't still in love with Christina's mother, Grace certainly wouldn't be on his radar.

Not that she could possibly be interested. She had college and a career to think about, after all. If that weren't enough, all she had to do was look at her mother's run of ruined relationships. Love—or what passed for love—rarely lasted.

Ryan's upturned gaze and quiet words nudged such thoughts aside. "You'd really give up your Sunday afternoon to ride all the way over to Shelby with me?"

Deciding it was time to lighten the mood, Grace wiggled a brow. "Only if you promise to take me to the amusement park and let me beat you at miniature golf."

Ryan grinned. "Have you seen me play miniature golf? Believe me, there won't be any 'letting' involved."

Sunday afternoon arrived both too soon and not soon enough for Ryan. He dreaded another uncomfortable encounter with the Burches, but spending the day with Grace sounded better and better all the time.

Shortly after twelve, he parked his pickup beside the Cross Roads Farm caretaker's cottage, careful not to bump Grace's silver-blue Yaris as he opened his door. "Stay buckled in, sweetie," he told Christina in the backseat.

"You called me sweetie because you think I'm sweet, right, Daddy?"

"That's right, sugarplum."

A faint smile pricked her lips, and his heart flipped. Getting a smile from her always did that to him. "I'll be back with Grace in a sec, okay?"

"But I want to see the horses. You should check Lady's shoe."

"Lady's shoe is fine. Besides, we have to get on the road pretty quick so you can have a good visit with Grandma and Grandpa Burch."

Christina mashed her lips together, her smile fading. "Horses are more intriguing."

Ryan had to bite the inside of his cheek to keep from chuckling at his pint-size thesaurus. "That well may be, but Grandma and Grandpa really want to see you."

Footsteps crunched on the gravel, and Ryan swiveled to see Grace marching over to the pickup. She looked smart in deep indigo jeans and a crisp white shirt beneath a cranberry-red blazer. She'd secured her mass of wavy hair into a ponytail at her nape, while a few loose strands fringed her forehead and temples.

Ryan's fingers suddenly itched with the need to wrap themselves around one of those curls. He shoved his hands into his pockets. "Hey, squirt. Ready to go?"

"All set." Grace leaned in Ryan's door to wave at Christina before rounding the rear of the pickup to reach the passenger side.

Torn between climbing in behind the wheel or following Grace to open her door like a gentleman, Ryan opted for the former. He'd always sensed that Grace—like Shana—wasn't real big on the whole "weaker sex" thing. Besides, they were just two friends out for the afternoon, right? No sense complicating things.

Ryan's life was complicated enough.

At least the hour-and-a-half drive to Shelby would give him a chance to rein in his festering annoyance before he faced the Burches. Minutes after hitting the highway, he was relieved when a peek in the rearview mirror told him Christina had drifted off for a nap. The visit would go much better if she weren't tired and grumpy.

Relaxing, Ryan glanced over at Grace, who had hardly spoken a word since they left Cross Roads Farm. "I thought you were supposed to keep me company this afternoon."

She angled him a halfhearted smile. "Sorry. My mind was on the classwork I need to make up."

"You should have said something. I'd have understood if you needed to bow out."

"I'll work on it tonight after we get back." Grace flicked her ponytail off her shoulder and gazed out the side window. "I wasn't in the mood for studying anyway."

"Tough time, I know." Ryan exhaled slowly and adjusted his grip on the steering wheel. *Lord, I'm really hurting for Kip and Sheridan. Please heal their sadness, and if it's Your will, bring them the child they're hoping for very, very soon.*

Somber silence hung between them for several long minutes, until finally Grace shifted in her seat. She reached across the console to poke Ryan's shoulder. "Hey, enough with the doom and gloom, okay? It's a gorgeous, sunshiny day, and we're two buddies out for a Sunday drive." She glanced over her shoulder at Christina. "Make that two and a half."

Ryan chuckled, more than glad for a reason to put unpleasant thoughts aside. "Yeah, we could pretend we're on our way to Disney World. You, me, and—"

He extinguished that image before he could complete it. The three of them were *not* a family. Christina's mom—the woman who *should* be sitting across the pickup from him—was clear on the other side of the world.

Grace cast him a gently accusing look. "You're frowning again. I thought we just agreed to look on the bright side."

"Yeah, sorry." He dredged up something resembling a laugh. No point dwelling on the fact that Shana would never be the mother Christina needed, much less Ryan's wife. No point hoping Grace or any other woman could possibly fall for an ex–bad boy raising a four-year-old with Asperger's. And definitely no point trying to explain a bunch of crazy, mixed-up feelings about life and love and unrequited hopes that sometimes made him want to run screaming into the night.

Somehow he managed to keep the conversation light as they continued on toward Shelby. But as they neared the Burches' home, his anxiety came barreling back. By the time he parked in their driveway, his stomach was in knots.

"Take a deep breath, Ryan." Grace must have noticed his hands clenching the steering wheel. "You need me to walk in with you?"

"No, it's better if you wait here." Clambering for a deep breath, he strove for a calm facade as he helped Christina out of her car seat and onto the sidewalk. "Got your backpack, sweetie?"

"Yes, Daddy." She shrugged into the shoulder straps. Her tiny eyebrows drew together as she stared up at him. "But Grandma and Grandpa don't like horses. They only like princesses and ballerinas."

The front door of the stately white two-story burst open,

and Mrs. Burch flew down the porch steps. "Christina, darling! We've been watching for you!" She scooped Christina into her arms and spun in a small circle.

Christina grunted, thrusting her hands against Mrs. Burch's shoulders. "Grandma, stop! You're making me dizzy."

Obliging with a reluctant sigh, Mrs. Burch patted Christina's head. "Grandma is just happy-happy-happy to see her little munchkin again."

Ryan's little girl shared a look with him that said her grandmother was a total fruitcake. Those weren't exactly the words Christina would have used, but the message was clear: *You're really leaving me here with this woman who can't even talk like a grown-up?*

Kneeling before Christina, Ryan tucked one of her brown curls behind her ear. He lowered his voice. "I'll be back for you in a couple of hours, okay? Can you handle it for that long?"

She nodded solemnly, and Ryan tweaked her chin as he stood. In the same moment he noticed Mrs. Burch scowling toward the pickup.

"I see you have a lady friend with you," she said, her tone icy. "Does Shana know you're seeing someone?"

"Grace is just a friend." *Not that it's any of your business.*

"You shouldn't confuse Christina. She has a mother, after all."

"Christina is not—" Ryan clamped his teeth together. Since Shana left for Afghanistan, the Burches seemed to have developed a blind spot about their relationship with their daughter, probably a sick combination of worry and guilt. They couldn't seem to admit it was their own self-centered, control-freak tendencies that had driven Shana away.

Regaining a measure of composure, Ryan edged toward the pickup. "You all have a nice visit. I'll be back at four o'clock sharp."

Chapter 4

Grace sensed Mrs. Burch's animosity the moment their gazes met. Clearly the woman didn't want anyone usurping her daughter's place in Christina's life. Or Ryan's, for that matter.

Well, she didn't have anything to worry about.

"You okay?" she asked as Ryan climbed into the driver's seat.

"Nothin' a couple rounds of mini golf won't cure." The set of his jaw belied the lightness in his tone. He started the engine and shifted into reverse.

As they backed out of the driveway, Grace watched Mrs. Burch lead Christina by the hand up the porch steps. Pausing at the threshold, the little girl turned and wiggled her fingers in a timid wave. Grace waved back. "Poor kid," she murmured. "Although she looks like she's handling the grandparent thing a whole lot better than her dad."

"Don't rub it in." Ryan slouched in the seat, one wrist

draped over the steering wheel as he started up the street. "Wanna stop for a burger before we hit the amusement park? I sorta skipped lunch."

Grace shot him a knowing smirk. "Too busy stressing out, were you?"

Ryan slanted her a look. "Those people are clueless. Utterly clueless. They're in denial about Shana, and they're in denial about Christina. They've never really tried to understand Asperger syndrome."

"They love Christina, though. I could see it in Mrs. Burch's face the moment she came out the front door."

"Love. That's rich. They don't know what love is."

"People express love in different ways, I guess." Arms crossed, Grace fell silent for a moment, thinking of her own mother. "And some people never get it right."

Ryan turned into the parking lot of a fast-food restaurant. "Hey, what happened to our moratorium on gloom and doom?"

"Good question." A huge poster on the restaurant window caught Grace's eye. She nudged Ryan's arm and pointed. "Buy me a super-size chocolate chip milkshake and I'll be one super-happy camper for the rest of the day."

His relaxed grin warmed her heart. "Deal."

Once Grace had finished her shake and Ryan had filled up on a double-decker bacon-cheddar burger and fries, they headed to the amusement park. Ryan turned out to be as lousy a miniature golfer as he'd claimed, and by the fifth hole Grace subtly began flubbing a few shots on purpose so he wouldn't feel so bad about losing to her.

A few minutes into their second round, she noticed Ryan checking his watch more frequently, and his putts grew even less accurate. As they waited on a bench while a family of five played through, Grace bumped Ryan's knee with her own. "Stop worrying. If things weren't going well, wouldn't they call?"

"Maybe." Ryan sighed. "Or maybe not."

"It won't be much longer. Before you know it, the day will be over and we'll be headed back to Kingsley."

Ryan reached for her hand. "This afternoon has sure been easier with you along. By myself, I'd have done a slow burn from the moment I dropped Christina off."

Heat filled Grace's chest. "What are friends for, huh?"

"Friends…yeah." Ryan sniffed. "Hey, you're up," he said, nodding toward the green. "Show me how it's done, 'Arnie.'"

Grace rose in mock indignation. She threatened to club Ryan with the handle of her putter. "Are you insinuating I resemble Arnold Palmer?"

"No way!" He waved his hands to ward off the fake blow. "You're *way* younger."

"Uh-huh. Glad you noticed." Rolling her eyes, Grace set her ball on the tee and prepared to line up a shot. The ball rolled cleanly between two boulders, up a slight incline, and onto the putting area, coming to rest within a foot of the cup.

"Nice shot." Ryan tossed his ball in the air and caught it with a snap of his wrist. "High time you gave me some pointers, don't you think?"

"Seriously?" Grinning, Grace cocked her head. "I thought you'd never ask."

Ryan set his ball on the tee and then took his stance. "So what am I doing wrong, coach?"

"Well, um…" Grace edged closer. "For starters, it's your grip."

"What's wrong with my grip?"

"You're holding a golf putter, not a sledgehammer." Grace moved beside him and demonstrated. "See? Left hand on top, right hand close up under the left, thumbs pointing down the shaft. And don't be so loosey-goosey with your wrists."

"Gotcha." Ryan shook out his arms and adjusted his grip. "What else?"

"Square your stance. Your shoulders should be parallel with the direction of your putt."

Ryan thrust one hand on his hip. "Wait a minute. I didn't realize mini golf required a degree in geometry."

Grace glared. "You want my help or not?"

"Okay, okay. Square stance. Parallel something-or-other." With a pained sigh, Ryan gripped his putter and stood over the ball. "Like this?"

"Not quite." Laying her putter aside, Grace chewed the inside of her cheek as she studied Ryan's position. "Your hips need to be…" Hesitantly she moved behind him and rested her hands on either side of his waist, turning his body until his hips lined up with the direction of the putt.

"Better?" Ryan's voice sounded husky.

"Much. Now, um, you just need to…" Why did her tongue suddenly stick to the roof of her mouth? "Just, um…"

"I'm guessing this is the part where I hit the ball." He cleared his throat. "Maybe you'd better show me."

"Right." Holding her breath, she reached around him until her palms rested on his forearms. "You want to pull back, tap the ball gently"—she guided his hands through the motions—"and keep your head down as you follow through."

When the ball rolled smoothly through the obstacles and missed a hole-in-one by mere inches, Ryan let out a whoop. He dropped his club and captured Grace in a one-arm victory hug. "Looky there, I'm a golfer!"

If Ryan's spontaneous display of gratitude wasn't enough to make Grace blush, the sudden burst of applause behind them certainly was. She freed herself from Ryan's embrace to see several teens cheering for them. What else could she do but smile and bow, then acknowledge her protégé?

One of the teenage boys sidled closer, a leering grin lighting his eyes. "If you're giving lessons, ma'am, I'd sure like to sign up."

Ryan stepped between Grace and her wannabe golf student. "Son, you can't afford the tuition." An edge crept into his voice. "Why don't you kiddies run along and play pat-a-cake while we finish this hole."

The teens backed off but not without scowls and a few mumbled gibes. Grace shot Ryan a scowl of her own. "What was *that* all about?"

Ryan stalked up the green and tapped his ball into the cup. "I didn't like the way that guy was looking at you."

Catching up, Grace sank her own ball, all the while trying to make sense of the crazy mix of awkwardness and delight coursing through her. She felt like a princess who'd just had a knight defend her honor.

Not that she needed defending from a pimple-faced teen, for crying out loud!

She set her ball on the next tee and then overswung, knocking the ball off course and into a pond.

Chuckling, Ryan scratched the back of his head. "That's gonna cost you."

"Like *you* have any room to talk." Grace marched over to the pond, knelt at the edge, and fished her ball out of the shallows. She extended her dripping arm out from her side as she tromped back to the green. Cringing with self-consciousness, she glanced at her watch. "It's getting close to four. Maybe we should stop and head back to the Burches'."

The moment she spoke the words, she wished she could take them back. The last glimmers of lightheartedness faded from Ryan's eyes as his earlier tension returned. He glanced away with a shrug. "Yeah, guess it's about that time."

If not for Ryan's urgency to hurry Christina away from the Burches, he could have happily spent the rest of the afternoon letting Grace teach him how to putt. Wouldn't take much effort to pretend he needed remedial work so she'd stand extra-close again. She was so easy to be with, not to mention easy on the eyes. No wonder that teenage hunk o' burnin' love was so anxious to sign up for private lessons.

"Ryan?"

Stopped at a red light, he glanced across the pickup console into Grace's thoughtful gaze.

She smiled. "I had fun this afternoon. I'm glad I came along."

"Me, too. We'll have to do this again sometime...*without* the pressure of dealing with the Burches." The light changed, and Ryan continued on through downtown Shelby.

"I'd love doing something fun with Christina, maybe take her to Carowinds or Discovery Place."

"The children's museum is more her style than the amusement park." Ryan pictured the three of them exploring the Discovery Place exhibits, and some of his anxiety dissipated. "Let's plan on it one of these weekends when you're free."

He smothered the wishful sigh begging for release. Maybe he'd been a fool all these years, staying faithful to a dream, holding out hope that Shana would come to her senses and marry him so they could make the home Christina deserved. Maybe it was time to take himself off the shelf and find a woman who could love him *and* his little girl, be the mom Christina needed.

He wouldn't mind at all if that woman were Grace, no doubt about it. If they hadn't drifted apart after high school, if he'd never fallen for Shana, who knew what might have developed between him and Grace? But for years now, she'd been giving off vibes that suggested friendship was as far as she'd take things. Maybe once she finished school and wasn't working herself to death commuting, studying, and holding down two part-time jobs.

But could he wait that long? The hollow place inside his heart told him no.

Turning onto the Burches' street, Ryan drew his thoughts away from impossible dreams and tried to steel himself for the inevitable face-off with Shana's parents. As he neared their house, he glimpsed a dark blue SUV parked near the mailbox.

Grace sat up straighter. "Looks like they have company."

A decal in the rear window caught Ryan's eye. When he recognized the five-point star, insignia of the US Army, his stomach clenched. He parked in the driveway and shut off the engine, hands trembling as he removed the key from the ignition.

Grace touched his arm, her gaze questioning.

"This doesn't look good." He swallowed, fought for breath, reached for the door handle. "I'd better go inside and find out what's happened."

"I'm going with you." She threw open the door, her feet hitting the driveway before he could protest.

Considering how his knees were shaking, he wasn't of a mind to argue. He knew how this stuff worked. They always came in person to give you bad news. *Oh, God, Christina's in there! Please, Lord, guard her precious little heart!*

The thought of what his daughter might be going through spurred Ryan forward. He took the porch steps two at a time and then hammered on the front door. An eternity passed before Harold Burch finally answered. Stoop-shouldered, his eyes swollen and red, Shana's father appeared to have aged ten years. Wordlessly he held the door for Ryan and nodded toward the living room.

Ryan paused in the archway, his gaze raking the room. A uniformed man and woman sat on the sofa across from Shana's mother, who wept into a handful of tissues. She glanced up at Ryan and shook her head.

The female officer rose and approached Ryan, and it was then he noticed the gold cross on her lapel. "I'm Chaplain Giusti. You must be Christina's father."

Ryan nodded. "Where is she?"

"In the kitchen. I just checked on her." The chaplain offered a sad smile. "Such a sweetheart. She's been drawing the most wonderful pictures of horses."

"Does she—" The words jammed in Ryan's throat. "I mean, did you tell her?"

"No. We thought it would be easier coming from you."

Easier? For whom? How was he supposed to tell his little girl her mother was dead? How was he supposed to believe it himself?

"Ryan." Grace's whisper was followed by the gentle touch of her hand. "Go talk with them. I'll stay with Christina."

He dipped his chin and tried to force the words *thank you* from his lips, but all he managed was a hoarse choking sound.

The chaplain took him by the arm. "Come sit down, Mr. O'Keefe. I know this must be a terrible shock."

Mr. Burch now stood behind his wife's chair, one hand absently massaging her shoulder. He slid a pained glance in Ryan's direction and then quickly looked away. His cheek muscles knotted. "I knew this would happen. I knew it all along."

Ryan allowed the chaplain to guide him to a chair, and all he could think was how ridiculous he must look, a blue-collar guy in jeans and sneakers perched upon salmon-pink velveteen. He'd never felt comfortable in the Burches' home. He understood why Shana never had, either.

"Mr. O'Keefe—"

"Ryan. Just Ryan." He slumped forward, hands clasped between his knees. "How… When?"

The other officer, a slender-faced black man, shifted to the end of the sofa closest to Ryan. He kept his voice low. "Corporal Burch was traveling in a Humvee with three other infantrymen when a roadside bomb exploded shortly after oh-seven-hundred yesterday, Afghanistan time. Two were killed instantly. The other two, including Corporal Burch, received extensive injuries and passed away en route to the field hospital."

Ryan hauled in a shaky breath. "So…she suffered."

"Medics were on the scene within minutes," the officer replied, his tone filled with compassion. "I can assure you Corporal Burch received the best possible trauma care and pain relief."

"What about her body?" Mrs. Burch said through a sob. "When can we have our daughter back?"

Ryan's head snapped up. *Now* they wanted their daughter back? What right did they have, after they drove her away? Before he voiced the angry words burning his tongue, he bolted to his feet. "I need to get Christina home." He looked to the chaplain. "Will someone call me when…when…"

She nodded. "Of course. As the father of Corporal Burch's daughter, you were listed as secondary next of kin. I promise, you'll be kept fully informed." Chaplain Giusti slid a business card into Ryan's hand. "Please feel free to call me anytime. I'm here to help."

Help. Right. Like the army would be there to hold his hand while he explained to Christina why her mother was never coming back. He slogged into the hallway, stumbling once on his way to the kitchen. *Oh, God, not Shana! Let this be a bad dream. You can't take Christina's mother!*

Chapter 5

"It was so sad. My stomach ached for Ryan." Grace stood with her arms laced across her abdomen as she watched Kip groom one of their newest horses, a chestnut gelding named Red, in preparation for the Tuesday evening riding-therapy class.

"Tough. Real tough." Kip lifted Red's left front leg and brushed a clump of dried mud off the horse's pastern. "Hand me the hoof pick?"

Kip might not say much, but Grace had learned to read his body language. The firm set of his jaw and his relentless concentration on the job at hand meant he was stuffing his feelings—as usual. Since Sheridan's miscarriage last week, he'd become even less communicative.

At least he didn't withdraw from Sheridan. No one could ask for a more attentive, concerned, supportive husband. Grace had seen the tender way Kip tucked Sheridan beneath his arm as they sat on the porch swing at the close of the day. She'd overheard his murmured words of comfort, his promise that the Lord would get them through this loss, just as He'd carried them through other tough times.

She knew also that, in spite of their pain, both Kip and Sheridan believed in God's mercies with all their hearts. Grace wanted to believe, too, but when God denied such a devoted couple the child they prayed for—when He allowed a sweet little girl's mother to die a tragic death—

Why, God? Why?

"Hello, you two." Filipa Cross strode through the barn door, guitar case in hand. About four months along in her pregnancy, she wore a loose knit top over stretchy jeans. Her long, black hair hung from a butterfly clip. "I saw Sheridan setting up in the arena. Should she be teaching so soon?"

Kip moved to Red's rear hoof. "Can't stop her. She'd rather keep busy."

Grace stepped around to the horse's head and stroked the white strip that ran from his nose to his forelock. "You're looking good, Fil. Over the morning sickness yet?"

"Much better. Sheridan told me I should try ginger tea, and…" Filipa's voice trailed off. She cast a regretful glance at Kip, who kept his face averted as he worked on the next hoof.

Two more volunteers entered the barn, and Grace smiled a greeting. Glancing back at Filipa, she said, "It's later than I thought. I should start getting Christina's horse ready."

"And I need to set up for the music therapy session." Resting one hand on her swelling abdomen, Filipa offered Grace an inviting smile. "Come over sometime. We're overdue for a nice, long visit."

"Love to, but with work and school and all…" She shrugged.

"You have to eat. How about dinner Friday after you get home from UNC?"

"Can I let you know later in the week?"

"Sure." With a parting wave, Filipa left the barn.

Entering Belle's stall with a grooming tote, Grace pondered why she'd hesitated at Fil's invitation. Nathan and Filipa lived less than half a mile away, having bought the Weber place after old Mrs. Weber passed away three years ago. It seemed fitting that they now owned the peach orchard where Nathan and Fil used to play hide-and-seek as children.

Maybe part of Grace's resistance had to do with the fact that nearly everyone else at Cross Roads Farm had a history together. Nathan and Sheridan had grown up here. Filipa's father, Manuelo Beltran, had been the stable hand for over twenty years, and their family lived just down the road. Kip may have come to work at the farm only months before Grace arrived, but by then he'd already fallen in love with Sheridan and had begun to think of Cross Roads Farm as home.

But no matter how hard both Kip and the Crosses had worked to make Grace feel that she belonged, she couldn't forget how her mother had dragged her away from their home and friends in Texas and dumped her into the laps of virtual strangers.

Oh, she wasn't complaining. Finding Kip and meeting the Crosses had definitely changed her life for the better. No telling what kind of trouble she might have ended up in if she'd stayed with her unstable, substance-abusing mother.

"Hey, little bit." Kip propped his forearm on the stall gate. "Sher's calling for the horses in the arena."

"Almost ready." Grace ran a hand along Belle's mane before straightening a fuzzy white saddle pad across the horse's back. "Have you seen Ryan and Christina yet? It's not like them to be late."

"Ryan probably got hung up at an appointment. They'll

be here." Kip handed her a child-size English saddle from the rack outside the stall. "Stirrup leathers on the eighth hole," he read from a tack chart.

"Already set." After buckling the girth, Grace released the stall tie and attached Belle's lead rope. Time to get her head out of the ether and down to business.

When she led Belle into the arena a few minutes later, concern tightened her stomach. Still no sign of Ryan and Christina. Had Ryan told his daughter about her mother? If he had, could she even understand?

Parked in his driveway after an extra-long day on the job, Ryan let his head fall forward to rest on the steering wheel. He released a ragged sigh.

"Daddy, I need my supper right now." A tiny hand tapped him twice on the shoulder.

Ryan glanced into the backseat to see that Christina had unbuckled herself and was standing behind him. "Yeah, sugarplum. I'm hungry, too."

Except he had no idea what to fix for supper tonight, much less the energy to think about it.

"It's Tuesday." She tapped him again. "Daddy, it's *Tuesday.*"

"Tuesday. Right." At least he thought so. He'd kind of lost track of time since Sunday. *Tuesday... Tuesday...* Groaning, Ryan checked his watch and then slapped himself on the forehead. "Aw, man."

"Come on, Daddy. It's Tuesday, so we have to eat supper at five o'clock because then we have to go to my class." Christina jerked on the rear door handle, which, as a safety precaution, was set to open only from the outside. She yanked harder. "Come *on*, Daddy! We eat at five o'clock!"

He sensed a meltdown in the works, and it would only get worse when he informed his precocious little girl it was already nearly seven and there was no way they'd make it to Cross Roads Farm for her riding class. Bracing himself, he stepped from the pickup and opened her door. "Now, sweetie—"

She lunged past him, backpack scraping up sod behind her as she dashed for the porch steps. "Hurry up, hurry up, hurry up!"

Lord, give me strength! Feet dragging, Ryan caught up and unlocked the back door. He'd just about steeled himself to sit down with Christina tonight and try to explain about her mother's death. Now he had serious second thoughts.

He knew he couldn't put it off much longer, though. Christina had grown accustomed to Shana's routine of checking in on video chat once a week, and she'd soon start asking when Mommy would call again. Spying Chaplain Giusti's business card where he'd laid it on the counter reminded Ryan of her phone call earlier. The Burches had arranged for Shana's funeral to be held Friday evening in Shelby—one more thing Ryan had to figure out how to explain to his little girl.

Rustling sounds from Christina's room drew his attention. First the closet door banged then a dresser drawer slammed shut. Something hit the floor with a foundation-rattling thud.

"Daddy! Daddy! Daddy!"

He tossed his keys onto the table and dashed through the house. Halting in Christina's doorway, he saw her bouncing on the mattress. "Christina Hope O'Keefe. What is going on in here?"

She pointed to the closet. Ryan stepped into the room, turned toward the open closet door, and let out an exasperated moan. Somehow—he couldn't even venture a guess—she'd tugged the clothes rod clean out of its brackets. All her clothes and hangers lay in a heap atop shoes, toys, and books.

Ryan couldn't think of a single thing to say. He simply stood there shaking his head while the acid that had been simmering in his belly all day slowly snaked up into his throat.

Behind him, Christina's bedsprings creaked in rhythm to her jumping. Her impatient "Daddy… Daddy… Daddy…" drilled a hole through his brain.

He lowered his head. His hands curled into two tight fists. "Christina. Stop. Right now."

"Daddy… Daddy…"

"I said *stop*!" He spun around, ready to grab her by the shoulders and force her to be still. He couldn't do this anymore, couldn't handle one more thing, couldn't—

The ringing of his cell phone jerked him to his senses. Breathing hard, he fumbled in his pocket until he freed the annoying little technological wonder. When he read Grace Lorimer on the caller ID, he closed his eyes for a moment and prayed he could answer with some semblance of composure.

"Hi, Grace," he said on his way out of Christina's room. Let her jump awhile longer. He really needed to calm down before he dealt with that situation.

"Ryan, are you okay? You sound…winded."

Air whistled from his nostrils. He plopped down on the sofa. "I've been better."

"I don't mean to bother you, but when Christina wasn't at class…well, I got a little worried."

"We're fine." *Sort of.* "Truth is I forgot what day it was. We haven't been home long." *Just long enough for both of us to completely lose our cool.* What was left of it, anyway.

"Oh." A pause. "I won't keep you then. I'll explain to Sheridan what happened."

Ryan felt lower than dirt. Not only was he letting down his little girl, he'd gotten so wrapped up in his own problems that he'd forgotten other people were hurting, too. "Did Sheridan teach today? I thought maybe she'd take some time off."

"She's doing much better. Anyway, she thrives on working with the kids."

"Two-sided therapy, I reckon." Ryan scrubbed his eyes with one palm. One ear tuned to the bedroom, he noticed the mattress springs had stopped creaking. "Look, I have a bummed-out four-year-old to deal with here. Then I gotta figure out some supper. Apologize to—"

"You haven't eaten yet? Neither have I. How about I pick up some Chinese for all of us?"

"I couldn't ask you to do that." But, boy, the offer sure sounded good. Ryan couldn't believe the sudden lurch of his heart at the prospect of not being alone tonight.

"It's no problem. I needed to come into town for groceries anyway."

"In that case, thanks."

Ending the call, Ryan collapsed against the sofa cushions. With Grace coming over, he should probably take a quick shower. Then, getting a whiff of his own body odor, with a little horse sweat and manure smell thrown in for good measure, he decided there was no *probably* about it.

But first he'd better check on Christina and try to make her understand why she'd missed another riding class. With luck, he *might* have her calmed down before Grace arrived.

Pushing up from the sofa, he realized a small part of him was actually grateful for all these distractions, because they were effectively keeping him from dealing with the one thing he couldn't bring himself to face: Shana's death.

Aromas of cashew chicken, sweet-and-sour pork, and pepper steak filled Grace's silver-blue Toyota Yaris. Unsure what Christina would like best, she'd selected a variety of entrées, plus a pint of wonton soup, six egg rolls, and both steamed and fried rice.

It was after eight by the time she arrived at Ryan's house—no doubt much later than they usually ate, so she hoped they weren't gnawing on the furniture by now. Grace, herself, was almost hungry enough to take a bite out of her dashboard.

Approaching the front door, arms loaded with waxy white paper sacks, she worked one finger free and pressed the doorbell. Seconds turned into minutes as she waited for Ryan to answer. She rang the bell again and was just about to go around back when the door jerked open.

Grace hardly recognized the harried man standing before her. Ryan's skin looked sallow under the porch light's amber glow. Dark half-moons bruised the hollows beneath his eyes. His sweat-stained T-shirt was streaked with something purple.

"Sorry," he mumbled. "I was, uh…" He motioned vaguely toward another part of the house.

She offered a worried smile and nodded toward the food sacks. "Um, where do you want this?"

As if coming out of a daze, Ryan blinked several times and then relieved her of the largest bag. "I'll need to clear off the table."

Grace followed him through the living room and into the breakfast area. Stunned by the disarray, she sucked in a breath. Milk spilled from an overturned glass next to a plastic plate that held what appeared to be a shredded peanut-butter-and-jelly sandwich. Blobs of grape jelly marked a trail from the table to the refrigerator door.

The grape jelly explained the purple smear on Ryan's T-shirt. Obviously he'd had an encounter with a very upset little girl.

"Oh, Ryan." Grace dropped her sacks on the only clean spot on the table. "You told her."

His forehead creased in a look of confusion. Then, his eyes clearing, he set the larger bag on the end of the counter. "Uh, no. We haven't gotten around to that yet. This," he said with a sweeping gesture taking in the jelly on his shirt and the mess on the kitchen table, "is the result of informing my darling daughter that she missed her riding lesson—again."

Grace pressed her lips together. "Oh, boy. Where is she now?"

"Asleep. Once I got her calmed down, she was out like a light."

"Poor thing." Grace tore off several paper towels and wet them under the faucet. "I'll clean the table if you'll dish out some Chinese. Because if I don't eat soon, I'll be throwing an adult-size tantrum. And believe me, it won't be pretty."

The frail chuckle that worked its way up Ryan's throat was music to Grace's ears. She made quick work of cleaning off the table, flushing the sandwich pieces down the disposal, and depositing the soiled place mats around the corner in the laundry room. By the time she'd wiped everything down with a clean paper towel, Ryan had heaped two plates high with food.

"There's sweet tea in the fridge," he said, setting the plates on the table. "You want to use the chopsticks, or should I get out some forks?"

"Forks, by all means!" Grace found two glasses in the cupboard. "I'm too hungry to fool with chopsticks."

"My sentiments exactly."

They said little for the next several minutes, all their energies focused on shoveling in the food. Ryan polished off five of the egg rolls after Grace insisted one was plenty for her. She offered him most of the wonton soup as well.

When they'd eaten all they could hold, Grace asked Ryan for a couple of plastic containers for leftovers. "There *might* be enough here if you and Christina want to warm it for lunch tomorrow, but I wouldn't guarantee it."

"Thanks again for bringing supper." Ryan rinsed their plates and set them in the dishwasher. He patted his belly with a satisfied groan. "I have to admit, life sure looks better on a full stomach."

Eyeing Ryan's T-shirt, which was now dribbled with dark brown soy sauce in addition to the jelly stain, Grace skewed her lips. "Life may look better, but that shirt is hopeless."

Ryan glanced down. "Oops."

"And, uh, I hate to say this, but…" Grace stepped back and fanned her hand in front of her nose. With the food aromas dissipating, she'd begun to get a good whiff of man sweat.

Ryan's face crinkled in an embarrassed grimace. "I was planning to shower before you got here, honestly. Then Hurricane Christina blew through."

"Why don't you go take one now while I finish in here?"

"Is that a suggestion…or an order?"

She raised one brow. "Whatever works."

While Ryan showered, Grace placed the remaining dishes in the dishwasher, added detergent, and started it. After wiping off the table, she searched in a kitchen drawer for fresh place mats. *Definitely a horse theme going on here.* This set featured a different breed of horse on each mat. Assuming Christina would like the bay quarter horse best because it looked the most like Belle, the mare she rode at Cross Roads Farm, Grace laid that mat at Christina's place.

She'd just settled on the sofa with one of Ryan's horse magazines when he ambled into the living room. His skin looked shiny and pink, as if he'd scoured with a steel-wool pad. His short hair stood up in wet spikes. Dressed in a fresh white T-shirt and clean jeans, he padded barefoot to the sofa. With a hesitant smile he said, "I wasn't sure you'd still be here."

"I wouldn't leave without saying good-bye." Grace laid aside the magazine, her gaze softening as she looked up at him. "Anyway, I thought you might need to talk."

Ryan pulled his lower lip between his teeth. "What if you stay but we don't talk? Would you be okay with that?"

A quiver started in Grace's abdomen. She braced both hands on the couch beside her hips and prepared to stand. "Ryan, if you think—"

"Sorry, that didn't come out right." With a pained laugh he sank into an easy chair and drew one hand across his unshaven jaw. "I just meant I'd like to chill with a friend for a while. Watch TV and zone out." His eyes fell shut. He dropped his head against the chair back and sighed noisily. "Honestly, I don't want to think or talk about *anything.*"

Grace exhaled slowly as her muscles relaxed. She should have known Ryan didn't have anything improper in mind. Only two days ago he'd learned the woman he loved, the mother of his child, was dead. Could there be anything more devastating? Yes, Kip and Sheridan also grieved, but at least they had each other…and they still had hope.

Spying the remote on the coffee table, Grace reached for it and turned on the TV. She flipped through stations until she found a sports channel—about as mindless a program as she could imagine—then scooted deeper into the sofa and put her feet up. Ryan was her friend, and he needed her. She'd stay as long as he wanted.

Chapter 6

"Daddy… Daddy… Daddy."

"You left me looooonely for yer love…"

Ryan forced his eyes open. With a country-western ballad blaring in one ear and Christina's strident voice in the other, it took him a few seconds to remember exactly where he was. He rolled over and slapped the Off button of his clock radio.

"Daddy, are you awake now?" Christina tugged on his T-shirt sleeve.

"Yeah, honey. Least I think so." Rubbing the sleep out of his eyes, he threw his legs off the side of the bed and sat up. A glance at the clock told him it was 7:28, almost a half hour past his scheduled wake-up time. If he didn't hustle, he'd be late for his first farrier appointment of the day.

Served him right for staying up so late last night. Staring bleary-eyed at the TV, straining to keep his mind a placid blank, he'd finally noticed around eleven that Grace had fallen asleep on the sofa. He'd considered getting a blanket and letting her stay over, but then she stirred. She insisted she was awake enough to drive home, but after she left, the emptiness threatened to swallow him whole. It took two more hours of mindless TV before he finally felt sleepy enough to go to bed.

"Daddy, get up. Make breakfast." His fully rested four-year-old spun on one toe and beelined for the kitchen.

Just deserts. Yep, just deserts.

With no time even for a shave this morning, Ryan yanked on jeans, boots, and a blue polo shirt, then poured juice and cold cereal for himself and Christina. Coffee would have to wait until he could stop at a convenience store later.

Then, as he stocked Christina's backpack with juice boxes, snack bars, and pudding cups, he glanced into the living room to see her perched on the sofa and staring at his laptop screen.

Drawing a slow breath, he stood across from her. "Whatcha doin', punkin?" As if he had to ask.

"Waiting for Mommy to call."

His chest caved. "Honey…"

"Today is Wednesday. Mommy often Skypes on Wednesdays." Christina scooted closer to the coffee table.

If his heart weren't breaking, he'd find this whole scenario laughable. Especially since the laptop wasn't even powered up, and Christina sat before a blank screen. He reached for her hand. "Come on, honey. Daddy's got to get to work. We'll…talk about this later."

She jerked away, fingers flicking faster than dragonfly wings. "I was sick when Mommy called last time. It's very important to be here when Mommy calls again."

Lacking the strength to deal with another meltdown, Ryan weighed his options. Occasionally when he needed a sitter, his neighbor Mrs. Airhart would watch Christina. Maybe he should call her.

Ten minutes later Mrs. Airhart stood at his front door, her little Pomeranian, Joy, tucked under her arm. "You saved my bacon, son," the white-haired woman said with a chuckle. "I was desperate for a reason to tell my book club I wouldn't be at the meeting this afternoon. The book they're discussing was so boring that I never got past the first chapter."

"Then I'm glad we could help each other out." Ryan showed Mrs. Airhart into the living room. He nodded toward Christina, who hadn't budged from her laptop vigil. "She could sit there for hours. No telling when—"

"Joy!" Christina scampered over to Mrs. Airhart and reached for the dog. Cuddling the furry creature under her chin, she crooned happily.

Ryan scratched the back of his head. "As I was saying…"

"My little Joy Bear has that effect on everyone." Mrs. Airhart tousled Christina's hair. "Hi, there, cutie. Mind if Joy and I visit with you awhile?"

"I'm waiting for my mommy to call. You can wait with me." Christina climbed onto the sofa again, giggling as Joy licked her cheek.

"Uh, Mrs. A, there's something you should know." Drawing his neighbor around the corner into the kitchen, Ryan quietly explained about Shana's death. "If I could impose on you again Friday evening, I really don't want to take Christina to the funeral. She just…wouldn't understand."

"Oh, son, I'm so sorry." Mrs. Airhart patted Ryan's hand. "Don't worry about a thing. Joy and I will take good care of Christina."

Hard work and plenty of it—the best way Ryan knew to keep his mind off his troubles. With each snap of the hoof nippers, with each hammer strike on the anvil, he put a little more distance between his heart and the hope-shattering blow he'd been dealt last Sunday. Knowing Christina was in Mrs. Airhart's competent care made it even easier to block out his worries. Otherwise, every trip to the pickup to check on Christina would have been one more reminder of the heartbreaking father-daughter talk he couldn't put off much longer.

At the end of the day, his back muscles screaming and his left foot throbbing after a Percheron landed its gigantic hoof on his big toe, Ryan put his tools away, locked up his trailer, and climbed wearily into the pickup cab. What he wouldn't give for a long soak in a burbling hot tub.

Limping through the back door at home, he found Mrs. Airhart running a dishcloth across the kitchen counter. Her eyes twinkled as she placed a finger to her lips and nodded toward the living room. There Ryan saw his little girl curled up asleep on the sofa. Mrs. Airhart's Pomeranian snuggled next to Christina, the dog's short, fox-like snout resting on Christina's arm and her luxurious red-gold tail fanned out across Christina's legs.

Ryan tipped back his ball cap. "How long has she been napping?"

"Nearly an hour, I'd say." Mrs. Airhart draped the dish-cloth over the faucet and motioned for Ryan to join her at the table. Her mouth creased in concern, she gently grasped Ryan's wrist. "She knows."

Meeting her gaze, Ryan cocked his head. "You mean… about Shana?"

A snow-white curl dipped across the woman's face as she gave a solemn nod.

"But how? You didn't—"

"No, son, I didn't tell her. I didn't have to." Mrs. Airhart glanced toward the sleeping child. "From what I gather, she's known all along."

"But she wasn't even in the room last Sunday. She couldn't have heard anything."

"Don't underestimate that bright little girl. She's more perceptive than you imagine." Mrs. Airhart sighed. "Your real problem, I'm afraid, will be helping her understand what she already knows is true."

Ryan rested his face in his hands. Christina's obsession with waiting for Shana's call today suddenly made perfect sense—a little girl's coping mechanism, pretending Mommy was alive and well and sure to call home soon.

Catching a motion out of the corner of his eye, Ryan lowered his hands and looked toward the living room. Christina yawned and stretched then sat up and pulled Joy into her lap.

"Hey, sugar." Ryan managed a tired smile. "Did you and Mrs. Airhart have a good day?"

"Pomeranians are good house pets. They're smart, and they don't eat much. I want a Pomeranian." Christina stroked the dog's silky coat. "We would need prescription food, though. Joy is on a kidney diet."

Mrs. Airhart chuckled. "Oh, sweetie, that's just because she's getting older. Not every dog needs special food."

Ryan pushed up from the table. "I should let you get home, Mrs. A. Can't thank you enough for all your help."

"My pleasure," she said, rising. "I figured you'd be too tired to think about supper, so I snooped in your fridge and pantry and whipped up a shepherd's pie. It can come out of the oven in another twenty minutes or so."

Only then did Ryan's brain connect with the aroma that had been teasing his senses since he walked in the door. "Wow. Thanks."

It took some convincing for Christina to let Joy go home

with Mrs. Airhart—and only after Ryan promised their neighbor would bring Joy over for another visit on Friday. In the few minutes before supper was ready, Ryan showered and changed then had Christina help him set the table.

As he handed her two plates from the cupboard, she said, "Daddy, you're walking funny."

"Mr. Wagner's big ol' gray draft horse stepped on my foot."

"Thaddeus?" Christina's tiny eyebrows drew together. She waggled her hands at her sides. "Percherons can weigh over two thousand pounds. Their hooves often reach eight inches across."

That, of course, was his fact-spewing daughter's way of telling him he had no business letting Thaddeus anywhere near his foot. That she cared about him. "Believe me, sweetie, getting stepped on wasn't part of the plan."

Ryan had examined his toe in the shower. It wasn't pretty. After supper he planned to prop his foot up with an ice pack. Tomorrow he should probably go to the clinic for an X-ray. He'd been stomped on before—unfortunately an occupational hazard—but this had to be the worst. The megadoses of ibuprofen he'd swallowed had brought little relief.

Mrs. Airhart's rich and meaty shepherd's pie temporarily took his mind off the pain. He could get used to coming home to supper in the oven every night. Then he looked across the table at the empty chair facing him and realized one very important part of the picture was missing—and now, always would be.

Aching loneliness swamped him, and the bite of food in his mouth turned to sawdust. He swallowed hard and laid aside his fork.

Christina stabbed a pea. "Mommy didn't call today."

It seemed pointless to tell her he'd never turned on the

computer. Edging his chair back, he rested an elbow on the table and frowned at his daughter. "Christina, do you understand why Mommy can't call you anymore?"

She turned her fork slowly and studied the pea. "Because there aren't any computers in heaven?"

An invisible knife sliced straight through Ryan's heart. His voice cracked. "You know your mommy loved you, right?"

Christina poked the pea into her mouth and then washed it down with a gulp of milk. "Mommy has brown eyes. I have green eyes, like you. Green is a good color."

That knife in his heart gave a sudden twist—Christina's special way of telling him she loved him. And nobody on God's green earth loved that kid like he did.

On Thursday morning Grace looked up from her computer screen to see Ryan standing at the check-in counter. "Hey, scuzzy."

"Hey, squirt."

Their greetings were spoken with none of the usual teasing tones but with an understated empathy. Grace glanced over the counter at Christina, who stood at her father's side. "This little one's not sick again, I hope."

"Nope. This time I'm here for myself." He shifted his weight, and the wince of pain creasing his face was unmistakable. "It's my foot. I think something's broken."

Grace rose to peer over the counter. Ryan's left foot was bootless, a dingy white tube sock peeking out beneath the hem of his jeans. "Oh, no. What did you do?"

He explained about the Percheron. "Can you work me in? I gotta get this seen to so I can get to work."

Grace quickly called the nurses' station, and a few minutes later Dr. Langston's nurse came to take Ryan to an exam room. "Leave Christina here with me," Grace said, opening a side door to admit Christina behind the counter.

Smiling his thanks, Ryan limped down the corridor.

"So what's new, kiddo?" Grace pulled an empty chair next to her own and helped Christina into the seat.

"My mommy was killed in the war. She can't Skype me anymore because they don't have computers in heaven." Christina glanced across the desk. "Daddy forgot my backpack. I need some paper. And two sharpened pencils, in case one breaks."

Processing the little girl's bluntness, Grace tried to keep her mouth from falling open while she pulled a few blank sheets from a printer tray and found two pencils in the desk drawer. "Here you go. I'll be right here looking over some files if you need anything."

How *did* a child like Christina deal with the death of a parent? It must be hard enough for Ryan to accept that Shana would never be in their lives again. But what about a little girl who would never really know her mother?

On the other hand, mothers weren't all they were cracked up to be. Grace's own mother was proof of that. So was Ryan's. And Shana's, if what Grace had heard was true. Maybe Christina was better off.

Then Linda Cross Jacobs's image filled Grace's thoughts. If only every child had a mother as loving and nurturing as Sheridan and Nathan's. From the day Kip brought Grace to live at Cross Roads Farm, Linda had welcomed her into her home and heart. The woman personified everything Grace believed a mother should be.

Everything Grace feared she herself could *never* be.

Permanently scarred. That's how she saw herself. Her first fifteen years—perhaps the most important years of her life—marred by the mistakes of her self-absorbed, alcoholic, hopelessly insecure mother.

A patient arrived to check in, and Grace welcomed the distraction. "Hi, Mr. Adams. Dr. Grundmann will see you in just a few minutes."

"No hurry." The elderly gentleman printed his name on the check-in sheet. Laying down the pen, he glanced over the counter, his eyes lighting up as he saw Christina. "I see you have a new receptionist on duty. Is she yours?"

"Oh, no. I'm just keeping an eye on her while her dad sees the doctor."

Christina scooted off her chair and tiptoed up beside Grace. "This is for you." She handed Grace a drawing.

Mr. Adams angled his head for a better look. "Goodness me, but you're a talented little artist, young lady. No guessing who that's supposed to be."

Studying the drawing, Grace realized Mr. Adams was right. From the long, curly ponytail to the dusting of freckles across a turned-up nose, clearly this was a picture of Grace. An unexpected tightness formed in her chest. "Honey, is this me?"

"My daddy told me I should draw pictures of Mommy so I can remember her better. But you have a ponytail so I drew you instead."

An embarrassed groan drew Grace's attention to the checkout window behind her. She swiveled her chair to see Ryan slumped over the counter and shot him a sympathetic smile. "My ponytail reminds her of horses. What can I say?"

Ryan merely shook his head as he slid the superbill across the counter.

Grace examined the codes and Dr. Langston's notation at the bottom. "Splinting of fractured phalanx and subungual hematoma drainage. Ouch."

"Sounds a lot worse when you put it like that." Ryan handed Grace his ten-dollar copay. "Problem is I'm supposed to keep my foot elevated for a day or two. Kinda makes it hard to shoe horses."

Grace rose to open the door for Christina and followed her out to the corridor. She caught Ryan's arm. "Give yourself a break, Ry. Taking a few days off might actually be a good thing."

"Wish I could, but…" Ryan's gaze drifted sideways, and he lowered his voice to a whisper. "Shana's funeral is tomorrow evening."

Grace's heart clenched. "Is there anything I can do?"

"My neighbor's gonna watch Christina. We'll be fine."

Somehow Grace doubted that. Watching Ryan limp toward the exit, his hand resting protectively on his little girl's head, Grace fought the urge to hurry after him and wrap him in her comforting embrace.

As a friend, of course. Only as a friend.

"Great chili, Fil." Nathan Cross reached across the dining room table to ladle another helping into his bowl. "How about you, Grace?"

She waved her hand. "It's delicious, but I'm still working on my first helping."

"Is it too spicy?" Filipa's eyes narrowed in a concerned frown. "I can be a bit heavy-handed with the jalapeños."

"No, it's just right. Remember, I grew up eating Tex-Mex." Giving a light laugh, Grace took another bite and tried to look as if she enjoyed the meal. But the simple truth was she was exhausted. As if work, UNC classes, and helping at the farm weren't enough, she'd spent too many sleepless nights lately worrying first about Sheridan and Kip, and now about Ryan and Christina.

Filipa gasped suddenly and pressed a hand against her abdomen. She chuckled softly. "Easy there, little one."

For a moment, Grace forgot her fatigue. "Is the baby kicking?"

Filipa and Nathan shared a look. "Yes, *she* is kicking," Filipa said with a knowing smile, "like the next Mia Hamm."

"She." A happy flutter filled Grace's chest. "You had an ultrasound?"

"This morning. We're having a girl!" Filipa reached for Nathan's hand, and the love reflected in their eyes seemed to light up the whole room.

Then Nathan sobered. "We haven't told Kip and Sher yet. Please don't say anything."

"I won't. I promise." Grace nibbled on a chunk of buttery cornbread. "Sher seems a lot better this week, though. A tiny bit more hopeful."

"I thought so, too." Inhaling deeply, Filipa picked up her spoon. "I just know when the time is right, God will give them a baby."

Grace wasn't so certain about God's involvement. If He really cared, wouldn't He have done something by now? Wouldn't He have done something about a lot of things that were going wrong in this crazy world?

"Grace?" Filipa touched her arm. "You look a million miles away."

She shook her head. "It's been a long week."

"You've seen a lot of Ryan lately," Nathan said. "How's he doing?"

"He's…coping, I guess. It's been hard. He's in Shelby tonight for Shana's funeral." Grace pushed chili around her bowl. She'd intended to call today and let him know she was thinking about him, but the time had gotten away from her.

"Ryan's blessed to have you in his life, especially now." A knowing smile curled Filipa's lips. "I always thought you two would get together someday."

Grace's brow furrowed. "I care about Ryan very much, but we're not *together*. We're just good friends."

"Nathan and I started out as best friends." Filipa's gaze slid to her husband, and they leaned toward each other to share a quick kiss. One hand resting protectively on her belly, Filipa smiled at Grace. "Take it from me. Friendship can be a *very* effective lead-in to romance."

"That definitely isn't the case with Ryan and me." Grace ignored the pinch beneath her sternum. "His heart has always belonged to Shana. If she hadn't been killed…"

Finishing his second helping of chili, Nathan pushed his empty bowl aside and leaned back. "Don't kid yourself. Shana was never the marrying kind. Not much of a mother, either, if you ask me."

Clearing her throat, Filipa shot Nathan a warning glance. "You shouldn't speak ill of the dead. Besides," she said, rising to clear the table, "it isn't our place to judge, especially knowing Shana didn't have the best parenting herself."

Exactly why Grace intended never to marry or have kids. What did she know about being a good wife and mother? For that matter, what did she know about true love?

She gathered up her bowl, spoon, and water glass. "Let me help with the dishes."

"Great. We can visit some more—*without* male ears listening in." With a tilt of her head, Filipa signaled Nathan toward the living room. "Go watch ESPN or something."

"A night off from KP? You don't have to ask me twice!" Nathan scurried across the hall.

While Filipa filled the dishwasher, Grace carried plates and bowls from the dining room. As she set the pot of leftover chili on the counter, Filipa handed her a plastic container. "Fill this for Ryan. I'm sure you'll see him before we do."

Ladling chili into the container, Grace gave her head an

annoyed shake. "If I didn't know better, I'd think you were trying to play matchmaker."

"You could do worse than Ryan O'Keefe." A thoughtful gaze creased Filipa's brow. "Be honest. You have feelings for him, don't you?"

"I told you, we're just friends."

"Mm-hmmm. Keep telling yourself that." Filipa snapped the lid onto Ryan's chili.

Grace's chest heaved with a tired breath. "You can't possibly understand, Fil. You and Nathan both come from wonderful families—loving parents, great brothers and sisters—"

"We've had our share of problems." Filipa started the tea-kettle and took two mugs from a cupboard. "Anyway, what does all that have to do with your having feelings for Ryan?"

"Everything." Grace sank into a chair in the breakfast nook. "I don't trust myself, Fil. I don't know if I could make a relationship work—with Ryan or any other guy."

Chapter 7

This relationship was *not* going to work.

Seething, Ryan flung his cell phone across the kitchen table. No matter how bad he felt for the Burches, there was no way he could take the afternoon off to run Christina over to Shelby. He'd tried to fend off their pleas as they left the cemetery last night, and now Shana's mom had phoned again this morning. Didn't they understand he had to work for a living? Because of his stupid broken toe, he was another two days behind on his farrier appointments.

The phone rang again, and Ryan nearly fell off his chair trying to reach it. When he read the caller ID—the Burches again—he almost didn't answer.

Hands fluttering, Christina toe-walked into the kitchen. "Daddy. I can't look for my purple socks. All this noise is *upsetting* me."

He'd sent her to her room to dress when the Burches called the first time. He had no intention of continuing this pointless conversation with Christina present. "I'm very, very sorry, sugarplum." He silenced the annoying marimba ringtone. "Why don't you go back to your room and shut the door? Daddy will come help you as soon as I get off this call."

Christina marched away in a huff. As soon as Ryan heard her door slam shut, he answered the call. "Look, Mrs. Burch—"

"It's *Mr.* Burch this time, and don't you dare hang up on me as you did my wife. She's still crying her eyes out over your gross insensitivity."

Ryan's stomach clenched. "I'm sorry, sir. I didn't mean to be rude. I tried to explain—"

"You think I want to hear your explanations? Have you no sense of how selfish you're being? Christina is all we have left of our Shana. We have every right to see our granddaughter."

"I'm not denying that, sir." Ryan gingerly lowered his sore foot off the adjacent chair. It would be a minor miracle getting a boot on, but he *had* to get back to work. "Like I tried to tell your wife, this afternoon just doesn't work for me. If you could wait till tomorrow—"

"If you won't bring Christina, we'll come and get her. And we're not settling for another of your miserly two-hour visits." Mr. Burch's tone grew even haughtier. "We've decided we want Christina for the entire week."

Ryan sucked air between his teeth before his temper exploded all over Harold Burch. "You don't know what you're asking. Christina needs her routine."

"Which is precisely why we want more time with her. How else can we establish a rapport so that she's comfortable with us?"

Please, Lord, make them understand. Ryan ground a fist into his eye socket. "I can't do it, Mr. Burch." Couldn't do it to Christina, couldn't do it to himself. He'd come to need that precious little girl like the air he breathed. "If you want to see Christina, it'll have to be another Sunday afternoon visit. Otherwise, it's a no-go."

"Humph. We'll see about *that*." Dead silence filled his ear.

Ryan laid the phone on the table then buried his face in his hands. *Was* he being selfish? Or only protecting his daughter from a situation destined to blow her routine to smithereens and guarantee a major meltdown…or worse?

Though the swelling had gone down, Ryan's broken toe still pressed hard against the inside of his boot. He adjusted his stance as he stood in his client's barn filing down a dappled mare's hoof. As if the aching toe wasn't enough, his brain continually replayed his phone conversation with Harold Burch.

Finishing with the mare, Ryan gathered up his tools and stowed them in the trailer. It was a few minutes past noon, and he'd been making good time so far. At this rate—and with no emergency calls—he just might cut his backlog in half before day's end.

Christina looked up from her sketchbook as Ryan climbed into the pickup. "I answered your phone, Daddy. Mr. Kip said to come over as soon as possible. Sundown's cracked hoof is worse."

So much for staying on schedule. "Did he say how bad?"

"Sundown is lame and needs immediate attention."

"All righty, then. Guess we're headed to Cross Roads Farm next." Checking to make sure Christina had buckled up, Ryan started the engine.

Then, as they turned at the next intersection, Christina stated matter-of-factly, "Grandpa and Grandma are coming to Cross Roads Farm today."

"What?" Ryan swung his head around to gape at his daughter. "Where'd you—"

A horn blared. Ryan faced forward in time to see a super-size SUV heading straight for him. Tires screeched as he swerved back into his own lane. He didn't even want to think about the crashing sound he'd heard coming from his trailer. Probably half his tools spilling onto the floor.

Once he'd regained control of both the pickup and himself, he tried again. "Sweetie, what makes you think Grandma and Grandpa are coming to the farm?"

"Grandpa told me."

Deep breath, deep breath. Ryan kept his eyes glued to the road as he asked, "You talked to him? When, honey?"

"After Mr. Kip."

"So you told him we'd be at Cross Roads Farm." Ryan swallowed the bile rising in his throat.

"Of course." Christina sighed in exasperation, as if her daddy couldn't be any more dense.

Yep, sometimes he wondered that himself. He'd been so proud of how competently his "little professor" fielded his calls while he carried on his work. Besides, it never occurred to him the Burches would have the gall to phone again. Hadn't he made his position crystal clear?

He had half a mind to stick to his appointment schedule and let Kip know he'd have to work Sundown in at the end of the day. Except he couldn't do that to a horse in pain, much less to his best friend. If the Burches did show up at Cross Roads Farm, Ryan would deal with them. What choice did he have?

He arrived at the farm as the big yellow bus from Pine Valley Haven headed out. Dave Williams, Ryan's former houseparent at the group home where he'd spent his teen years, tapped the horn and waved from the driver's seat. Waving back, Ryan pulled over to the side of the lane until the bus passed. Then, his eyes peeled for any sign of the Burches' fancy silver sedan, he parked the pickup next to the barn.

Whew. So far, so good. Maybe he could finish with Sundown and be out of here before they showed up. He shoved open his door. "You stay here, sweetie. Eat your sandwich if you're hungry."

Nose buried in her horse book, she did little more than nod.

Tipping his ball cap to a couple of departing volunteers, Ryan meandered into the barn and over to Sundown's stall. The big brown horse hunkered in the back corner, his head lowered and his weight shifted to relieve the pressure on his right front hoof.

Ryan eased into the stall. "Poor guy. I thought we had this crack under control."

"You know Sundown." Grace's mellow voice sounded behind him, and he turned to see her smiling over the stall gate. "He's had foot trouble ever since I've known him."

"Yeah, probably because you spoil him rotten." Tossing her a grin, Ryan ran gently probing fingers around Sundown's fetlock and down to the pastern and coronet. The horse snorted and flinched. "Pretty sore, aren't you, boy?"

"Can you help him?"

Straightening, Ryan rubbed his chin. "We can epoxy the crack and try a different type of shoe. You still giving him the hoof supplements I recommended?"

"Faithfully." Grace opened the gate and brought in Sundown's halter and lead rope. "Want him in the cross ties?"

"Thanks. I'll get some stuff from my trailer." He cringed to think what he might find back there after his near-miss on the road.

And that reminder brought the Burches slamming into

his thoughts. A twinge in his gut, he stopped at the pickup cab to check on Christina. "Honey, you doin'—"

She wasn't in her car seat. She wasn't anywhere to be seen.

"Christina?" Ryan yanked open the rear door and leaned into the cab, foolishly craning his body to look beneath the seats as if his little girl could possibly be hiding there. "Christina!"

"Ryan, what's wrong?" Grace came up behind him.

Breathing hard, he stood beside the pickup and mindlessly slapped his ball cap against his thigh. His gaze swept the area outside the barn. "She *knows* she's not supposed to get out of the truck."

"Take it easy. She can't have gone far." Grace marched around the pickup and toward the arena. "Christina?"

Still frozen in his tracks, Ryan could imagine only one possibility. The Burches had come. They'd snatched Christina right out from under his nose. *God, no—please, no!*

"Christina, are you out here?" Grace unlatched the arena gate and crossed over to the empty bleachers. No sign of the little girl anywhere.

Kip appeared from the small storage room behind the bleachers. "What's up?"

"Christina's missing. Ryan left her in the pickup, but she's not there." Glancing over her shoulder, Grace saw Ryan striding along the pasture fence line, his gaze intense as he searched for his daughter.

Just then a car drove up—a pricey-looking silver sedan. The driver braked even with Ryan, and the look of rage on Ryan's face as he marched around to the driver's door made Grace's stomach twist. A man stepped from the car, and Grace immediately recognized Harold Burch. Then she made out Mrs. Burch in the passenger seat. "What are *they* doing here?"

As she started forward, Kip grabbed her elbow. "Best you stay out of it."

"If this has anything to do with Christina—"

"Uh, sis…" Kip angled his head toward the back pasture.

Following his gaze, Grace spotted Sheridan and Christina walking hand in hand along the lane. Xena, Sheridan's big black Great Dane, pranced beside them. "Sher!" Grace loped out of the arena and met them as they approached the barn. She fell into step beside them and tried to keep her voice level so as not to alarm Christina. "Sher, did you take Christina out of the pickup?"

"Oh, no, has Ryan been worried?" Sheridan clapped a hand to her forehead. "I'm sorry! I stopped to say hi to her, and she wanted to pet Xena. We just took a short walk around the barn."

Christina patted Xena's head. "Great Danes are one of the largest breeds. Xena can't sit on my lap, but Joy can. Joy is a Pomeranian. She only weighs five pounds."

"That's nice, honey." The little girl's words barely registered. Nearing Ryan's pickup, Grace focused all her attention on the escalating argument between Ryan and Mr. Burch. She drew Sheridan to a halt and lowered her voice. "Keep Christina here, okay?"

Sheridan glanced toward the silver sedan. "Who is Ryan talking to?"

Before Grace could reply, Christina began bouncing on her toes, hands flapping, her tiny eyebrows drawn together. "I need to get in the pickup. I'm not supposed to be out of the pickup."

Grace and Sheridan shared a look before Grace jogged toward Ryan. He and Mr. Burch were so intent on yelling in each other's faces that they didn't notice her until she stepped between them and physically forced them apart. "Stop it, you two! You're acting like a couple of playground bullies."

"He's lyin' to my face!" Ryan's shoulders heaved. "Says he has no idea where Christina is."

A vein throbbed in Mr. Burch's forehead. "You irresponsible lout! You lost your own child, and you accuse *me*—"

"Just shut up. Christina's fine. She's *fine*." Grabbing both men by their upper arms, Grace wrestled them around until they faced the barn. "See? She's right there."

Ryan's relief was palpable. The bicep muscle beneath Grace's grip suddenly grew lax, and all the air whooshed from his lungs. He broke free of her grasp and ran straight for his daughter then swooped her into his arms and buried his face in her shiny brown curls. "Honey, where have you been? I told you not to leave the pickup."

Grace didn't realize she still held fast to Mr. Burch's arm until he harrumphed and jerked loose. "That man has no business raising a child. I'll see my granddaughter removed from his custody if it's the last thing I do."

Panic stabbed Grace's heart. She swung around to meet Mr. Burch's determined glare. "You can't mean that. Ryan's a great dad. Christina's his whole life."

Mrs. Burch's whimpering sobs sounded from inside the car. "Harold, let's just go home."

"No, Irene." Gaze fixed on Ryan and Christina, Mr. Burch took several halting breaths. "We drove all the way over here to see our granddaughter, and that's what we're going to do." Then, pulling a hand down his face, he returned to the car and leaned in the open door. "It'll be all right, sweetheart," he soothed. "Pull yourself together. I'll take care of this."

"Mr. Burch, please." Grace blocked his path. "Think of

what your arguing does to Christina. Don't make the situation worse."

As if seeing her for the first time, Mr. Burch tilted his head to angle Grace a contemptuous frown. "Do you think we came here intending to cause a scene? We're grieving, young lady. Can't you see that?" His frown became an anguished grimace. "We buried our only child last night. All we're asking is the comfort of spending time with our granddaughter."

"I feel for you; I really do." Compassion replaced Grace's earlier panic. "But Ryan's grieving, too, and so is Christina, in her own way. Ryan only wants what's best for her. If you'd both try a little harder to understand each other—"

"Don't lecture me about understanding!" The man's jaw trembled. He drew in a shaky breath. "For the rest of our lives, my wife and I will live with regret over the time we lost with Shana. Christina is our only chance to make things right."

"Then start today. Try working *with* Ryan instead of against him."

A motion caught Grace's eye as Ryan drew up beside her. With Christina tucked against his hip, her arms wrapped around his neck, he edged forward. "Mr. Burch, I'm sorry for everything I said. I was out of my head with worry."

"No doubt you were." Mr. Burch stiffened, but as he looked up at Christina, his expression softened into a grandfatherly smile. "I admit I overreacted as well. If we could just have a little time with our granddaughter…"

Ryan's mouth flattened. "I told you I have to work today. I'll bring her over tomorrow like I promised."

Sensing the men were about to unleash another verbal attack, Grace grappled for a peaceful solution. She pasted on her most persuasive smile. "Ryan, why don't you let Mr. and Mrs. Burch visit with Christina right here while you go on your appointments this afternoon? They can make themselves at home in my cottage, take a walk around the farm, whatever they like."

"I don't know…" Doubt simmered behind Ryan's eyes as he snuggled Christina closer.

With a pleading gaze, Grace turned Ryan aside and murmured, "Think about it. Christina loves the farm. She's in familiar surroundings, and Sheridan and I will both be nearby. What better place for them to visit?"

Biting his lip, Ryan chucked Christina under the chin. "Would you be okay with that, sweetie?"

She nodded. "But…I can't answer your phone and take messages."

"I think I can handle it for one afternoon." The smile that teased Ryan's lips lifted Grace's heart. With a resigned sigh he lowered the little girl to the ground. "You can tell Grandma and Grandpa all about the horses."

As Mr. Burch helped his wife from the car, Grace looped her arm through Ryan's. She felt his body grow rigid when Christina took her grandparents' hands and led them toward the front pasture, where Radar, Gem, and Red grazed. Already Christina was spouting details about each horse's background, coloring, size, and diet.

Ryan whistled softly. "She's somethin' else."

"She sure is." The warmth of his arm against her side elicited a tiny tremor in Grace's abdomen. Probably just a letdown after the showdown. She wouldn't let herself even consider the possibility Filipa had hinted at last night.

As if to convince herself, she gave Ryan's arm a friendly pat as she put some space between them. "Hadn't you better get to work on Sundown's hoof?"

A week and a half later, Ryan beamed with pride as he watched Christina rein Belle through the trail course at her Tuesday evening riding class. Sheridan had created a challenging course, having the riders weave around traffic cones, halt in a box and make a quarter turn, step over a series of ground poles, and back their horses through an L.

A tiny four-year-old negotiating the course with only minimal direction from her sidewalker and horse leader? That said plenty about how therapeutic riding helped develop both Christina's reasoning skills and her self-confidence.

Ryan's self-confidence, on the other hand, left a lot to be desired, especially after the Burches had shown up at Cross Roads Farm two Saturdays ago at the very moment he'd been searching frantically for Christina. Ryan hated to think how much worse the encounter could have been if not for Grace's intervention.

As it was, he'd been struggling with guilt ever since. Maybe the Burches were right. Maybe he wasn't being a responsible father by taking Christina along on his farrier calls. But the thought of leaving her in day care forty-plus hours a week made him physically sick.

"Hey, scuzzy." Grace dropped onto the bleacher seat beside him.

He looked up in surprise, tamping down an unexpected quiver in his stomach. "Hey, squirt. I was wondering about you when I saw a sub leading Christina's horse."

"I have two papers due tomorrow, plus a psychology test." Grace yawned and stretched one leg across the bench below them. "I needed a break, so I thought I'd see how the class is going." Giving Ryan the once-over, she added, "Christina is obviously doing a whole lot better than you."

"Yeah, well, maybe that's one big advantage to having Asperger's. She's totally focused on her own little world, while I have to deal with the grandparent fallout."

Grace shot him a worried frown. "Did something else happen?"

"Nothin' new. But the Burches sure don't hide their feelings about my qualifications as a parent." Ryan whipped off his ball cap and ran his thumb across the bill. "We went over to Shelby again last Sunday, and they were all over my case."

Shifting sideways to face him, Grace grumbled in annoyance. "What now?"

"They think Christina should be in a special school." Ryan watched his daughter ride up to a tall pole and drop three colored rings over the top. When Sheridan cheered and gave Christina a high five, Ryan asked, "Tell me, how can any special school do more for her than what she's getting right here?"

Grace sat silent for a moment before replying softly, "She won't be four years old forever, Ryan. Eventually she *will* need more than a weekly therapeutic riding class."

"I know that, okay?" Ryan slapped his ball cap back on his head. He'd heard Grace's unspoken reminder, too, that there'd soon come a time when his perennial take-your-daughter-to-work days would have to end.

But not yet, Lord. Let me keep her close awhile longer. Please.

Later, with Christina bathed, in her jammies, and tucked into bed, Ryan collapsed into his easy chair. When he closed his eyes for a moment, Grace's image flickered behind his eyelids. He knew she was right—it wouldn't be long before Christina would need a whole lot more than Ryan could offer.

Amazing how he could hear the same truth out of Grace's mouth with a completely different attitude than when it came from the Burches. Grace had a way about her, always had. Good with horses, good with kids...good with Ryan.

An aching hunger rippled through him, a sober reminder he was more than just a dad, more than just a working man. He was a man lonely for companionship, for the love of a good woman willing to stand beside him whatever came their way.

For years he'd held out hope that woman would be Shana. Hard to give up the dream of making a home with the mother of your child. But now that she was gone—really gone—maybe he could finally let her go and move on, open his heart to someone new…or someone who'd been there all along.

Grace…

Shaking himself back to reality, Ryan reached for the stack of bills and ads that had come in today's mail. Didn't need vinyl siding, didn't need a chimney sweep, sure as all get-out didn't plan on purchasing any mountaintop land in Tennessee. He'd handle the utility and credit card bills tomorrow.

He almost tossed the next piece of mail without opening it. Looked to be a solicitation from some ambulance-chasing lawyer's office in Charlotte. He slid his thumb under the envelope flap and tugged loose the single sheet of paper.

As he skimmed the first paragraph, his stomach bottomed out. Was this some kind of sick joke?

He read on and knew it was no joke.

The Burches were suing for custody of Christina.

Chapter 8

Pastor Wolfe might be the best preacher around, but Grace had a difficult time focusing on his sermon today. She believed intellectually that God loved her unconditionally, and she accepted what a privilege and blessing it was that God claimed her as His child. But she still felt distant from God, as if she could never really know Him, never experience true closeness with the "Abba, Father" Pastor Wolfe spoke about.

Thoughts of fathers and families brought Ryan to mind, and Grace found herself replaying their conversation last Tuesday during Christina's riding class. Ryan tried so hard to be a good dad. Why couldn't Mr. and Mrs. Burch see that?

And, good dad that Ryan was, since Grace didn't see Ryan in church this morning, she guessed he'd given up another Sunday so the Burches could spend more time with their granddaughter. Knowing how hard these trips to Shelby were for Ryan, Grace wished she'd offered to keep him company again. On the other hand, it was probably best she didn't intrude. For Christina's sake, Ryan and the Burches needed to work out their differences on their own.

After church, Grace joined Kip, Sheridan, Nathan, and Filipa for lunch at Kingsley Station, the train depot–themed restaurant in downtown Kingsley. Grace couldn't help noticing Filipa found it a little harder to squeeze into the round corner booth where they usually sat—or the fact that Sheridan made a point of *not* noticing.

When the server had taken their order, Sheridan excused herself to go to the ladies' room.

Grace scooted out of the booth behind her. "Mind if I tag along?"

"I'd go, too," Filipa said with a groan, "except it was hard enough getting *into* the booth."

Sheridan's attempt at a sympathetic chuckle didn't fool Grace. With a light touch to Sheridan's elbow, she prodded her toward the ladies' room.

As they washed their hands a few minutes later, Grace eyed Sheridan in the mirror. "You okay?"

Sheridan dropped the used paper towel into the waste container and angled Grace a crooked smile. "Kip and I are trying again."

Grace slipped an arm around her sister-in-law's waist and squeezed. "Are you sure you're not putting too much pressure on yourselves?"

"I know what you're saying. Every disappointment makes it even harder to stay hopeful." After returning Grace's hug, Sheridan checked her reflection and smoothed a stray wisp of short blond hair. "But I can't stop hoping. We want kids so badly—Kip especially. Becoming a dad means everything to him."

"He'll be a good one, I know." Grace released a soft sigh

as memories of her first years at Cross Roads Farm floated to the surface. "He sure took good care of me."

"And he loved every minute of it."

"After all the trouble I caused him?" Grace snorted a doubtful laugh.

Sheridan laughed with her. "I admit, you had your moments, but Kip and I are both so proud of the woman you've grown into."

Heat shot up Grace's neck. Before she turned any redder, she reached for the door handle. "We should get back before the guys send out a posse."

"They're probably so busy talking riding center business that they haven't even missed us." Sheridan stepped through the doorway, her smile turning wistful. "My dearest hope is that God will allow Kip and me to pass along the Cross Roads Farm legacy to a child of our own. Can't you just see Kip teaching his own little boy all about horses?"

Grace nodded, unable to speak over the sudden catch in her throat. As long as she lived, she'd never forgive her mother for denying her the right to know her own father—a man Kip described as patient, thoughtful, and loyal to a fault, a rough-and-tumble rodeo champ but a gentleman in every sense of the word, and the best horseman Kip had ever known.

If only Grace had been raised by her father, if only she'd grown up knowing that kind of love, that kind of stability. It hurt all the worse when she found out her dad had died not long after her mother left him…that he'd died before ever learning he had a daughter.

Arriving at their table, Grace immediately noticed the somber mood. As Kip stood so that she and Sheridan could slide into the booth, she asked, "What's going on?"

Kip fingered his cell phone, which lay on the table beside his iced-tea glass. "Ryan just called. Sounded real upset."

Grace's stomach heaved. The only people capable of *really* upsetting Ryan lately were the Burches. "What did he say?"

"Just that he had a problem and needed some advice. I'll head over to his place soon as we finish lunch."

Filipa patted Grace's arm. "Nathan and I will take you and Sheridan home."

As Grace opened her mouth to protest, the server arrived with their food. The Asian chicken salad Grace had been so hungry for ten minutes ago now looked unappetizing.

"Let's pray for Ryan," Nathan said. When everyone had joined hands, he continued, "Heavenly Father, we don't know what's going on with our friend Ryan today, but we know You're watching over him. Like Pastor Wolfe reminded us this morning, You are our Abba, our Daddy-God, concerned about every detail of our lives. So whatever Ryan needs, Lord, we're trusting You to provide."

After a chorus of amens, the table grew quiet except for the rustle of paper napkins and the clink of flatware against plates. Grace certainly wasn't in the mood for pleasant conversation. Kip was obviously worried, too, because he rammed his buffalo burger into his mouth as if he couldn't finish quickly enough.

Leaving most of his french fries untouched, Kip pushed his plate aside and reached for his Stetson on the window ledge. He drew Sheridan close for a quick kiss. "I'm gonna take off, honey. See you at home later."

"Kip, wait." Grace dabbed her lips, crumpled her napkin, and gathered up her purse. "Let me go with you. Please."

Kip's mouth flattened. "Don't know if that's a good idea, sis."

"If you guys are having a serious talk, Ryan won't want Christina overhearing. I can keep her company." Restless to get going, Grace nudged Sheridan to let her out of the booth.

"Give Ryan our love," Sheridan said before taking her seat again. "And call if there's anything we can do."

Minutes later, buckled into the passenger seat of Kip and Sheridan's sea-green SUV, Grace knotted her fists as she stared through the windshield. *God, if You really do love us like the pastor said, if You really do care—*

Then what? He'd miraculously mend the relationship between Ryan and the Burches? Give Kip and Sheridan the baby they so desperately wanted?

"What do you want from Me, Grace?"

The question so stunned her that for a moment she couldn't breathe. *I want... I want to know You're real.*

This can't be real. Can't be happening. God, please!

Ryan paced at the front window, one hand absently kneading the back of his neck. If Kip didn't get here soon, he'd crawl right out of his skin. The letter from the Burches' attorney lay flattened and creased and tucked away in his wallet behind his driver's license, the one place he felt certain Christina wouldn't accidentally come across it. Not that she could read that well, much less understand what the letter meant, but he wasn't taking any chances.

And, stupidly, he thought if he ignored the letter long enough—better yet, if he consented to giving the Burches all the visits with Christina he could arrange—they'd drop this whole custody issue.

So yesterday, after finishing the day's appointments, he'd called the Burches. "Uh, hi, this is Ryan," he'd said when their answering machine picked up. "Look, I know we've had our differences, and I really want to change that. I can bring Christina over tomorrow, and..."

This next part about killed him, but he'd squeezed his eyes shut and pressed on. "I'll...I'll let her stay the week if...if that's what you want... Call me. Okay?"

It was nearly eleven last night when Mr. Burch finally returned the call. "It's too late, Ryan," he said. "We're pursuing the custody case. Don't contact us again. All further communication will go through our attorney." A pause, while Ryan fought for breath. "I suggest you hire an attorney as well."

Hire an attorney? The thought that he even needed one tied Ryan's insides in knots. Forget getting any sleep. He'd tossed and turned most of the night trying to figure a way out of this living nightmare. Then this morning he'd had to explain to Christina why she couldn't go to her Sunday school class—"Because Daddy had a bad night, sweetie. I'm just too tired to make it to church today."

Which was a cryin' shame, because he needed God more than ever. Only the Lord could show him a way out of this mess…or were the problems Ryan faced today his due punishment for one night of unbridled teenage passion five years ago?

His faith told him that wasn't how God worked. *Therefore, there is now no condemnation for those who are in Christ Jesus,* Paul wrote in Romans. No condemnation, no punishment…but definitely consequences.

Ryan glanced toward the kitchen table, where Christina sat with her sketchbook copying the names of horse parts onto her colored-pencil drawing of a palomino. Christina, a *consequence*? No way! She was the true blessing in all this, and he'd be hanged if he let the Burches take her away from him!

Car doors sounded from the driveway. Ryan stepped onto his front porch to see Kip striding up the walk, Grace right behind him. Ryan slicked a nervous hand through his hair. "Wasn't expecting both of you."

Kip offered a brotherly smile as he joined Ryan on the

porch. "Grace offered to sit with Christina while you tell me what's got you so bothered."

"Good idea." Grateful relief poured through Ryan. He pointed Grace toward the kitchen. "Have her show you her latest sketches."

Grace paused next to Ryan on her way into the house. "Hang in there. Whatever's going on, your friends have your back."

Too moved to speak, Ryan nodded his thanks. When the front door closed behind Grace, Ryan sank onto the top porch step and motioned for Kip to join him.

"So what's goin' on?" Kip asked as he settled onto the step.

With a groan, Ryan launched into an explanation about the custody suit and his futile attempt last night to appease the Burches. "I'm sunk, Kip. Shana's parents have money for high-priced lawyers. I don't. How am I gonna fight this?"

Kip peeled off his Stetson and propped it on one knee. "I thought you and Shana agreed to joint custody. Since she's gone, don't you have a paper that says Christina's yours now?"

"Yeah, I guess so. But if the Burches can convince some judge that I'm an unfit parent—"

"That'll never happen."

Ryan's chin fell to his chest. He let out a long, pained sigh. "You don't know that, Kip. You don't know the Burches. Once they set their mind to something, they usually get it."

Grace tried to refrain from eavesdropping, but her concern for Ryan got the better of her. Since Christina seemed perfectly content working on her sketch, Grace meandered over to the living room window. Staying out of sight behind the curtain, she tuned one ear in to the conversation between Ryan and Kip on the front porch—and nearly choked when she caught the gist of their discussion.

The Burches wanted to take Christina? How could they be so cruel?

The real question was how could *God* be so cruel?

Veins pulsing with anger, Grace swung away from the window. There had to be a way to stop this idiocy, some way to keep Ryan and his little girl together. Common sense told Grace it was too early to assume the worst. The Burches had to prove their case, didn't they? And *that* would never happen. They'd never in a million years convince a judge that Ryan was a bad father.

Those thoughts easing her mind somewhat, Grace inhaled several calming breaths. They were panicking for nothing. Ryan would get a good lawyer who'd prove the Burches didn't have a leg to stand on, and this whole mess would be forgotten.

Another deep breath and Grace felt calm enough to paste on a cheery smile for Christina. She marched into the kitchen and sank into the chair next to Ryan's little girl, noticing she'd turned to a new page in her sketchbook. "That's a cute doggy picture. What's the dog's name?"

"This is Joy. She's a Pomeranian and weighs five pounds. Joy lives next door with Mrs. Airhart." Christina added a few more wisps to Joy's fluffy tail. "Grandma Burch is getting me a dog like Joy."

"Really?" Grace lifted a brow. "She said so?"

"Yes, when she visited me at Cross Roads Farm. Grandma is going to keep my dog at her house so I can play with it there." Studying the drawing, Grace added two whiskers to the dog's nose.

A chill ran up Grace's spine. Did the Burches think they could *bribe* Christina into wanting to live with them?

The front door clicked, and seconds later Ryan and Kip ambled into the kitchen. "How's it going in here?" Ryan asked, his tone falsely bright.

"Christina's making a picture of the little dog next door." Grace stood, tension lacing her own voice. "How about you guys? Everything okay?"

"Better than an hour ago, thanks to your big brother." Ryan clapped Kip on the shoulder and exhaled tiredly. "I could use a soda. How about y'all?"

"Thanks, but we should get goin'." Kip lowered his voice. "You call that number I gave you first thing tomorrow. This'll be over before you know it."

They said their good-byes, and Grace climbed into the SUV with Kip. "I listened to some of what you said on the porch," she confessed as they drove away. "There's no chance the Burches could win custody, is there?"

Kip gave her a look that said he wasn't the least bit surprised by her eavesdropping. "I'm no lawyer, but seems to me this would be a hard fight for them to win. I gave Ryan Stan Turner's name and number."

"Tracie Turner's dad, from the Thursday morning class? I forgot he was an attorney." A tiny shiver of relief worked through Grace's limbs. At least Ryan wouldn't fight this battle without allies. Staring out the side window, she watched the flicker of sunlight on storefronts as they drove through downtown Kingsley. "This could get expensive, though, couldn't it?"

"Sure could." Kip turned left on the road out of town. "Let's just pray the Burches back off before it goes that far."

A sick, hopeless feeling festered deep in Grace's stomach. She shifted her gaze to her brother's solemn profile. "I don't know if I can pray, Kip. I'm not sure I believe God is listening."

Kip reached across the console to grasp her hand. "Don't

talk like that, sis. Of course He's listening. God always hears our prayers."

"Yes, but…He doesn't always answer them."

"What you mean is He doesn't always say yes." Returning his hand to the steering wheel, Kip firmed his mouth. His Adam's apple worked, pretty much the only emotion Grace's brother ever showed. "But I gotta believe God always knows best, even if it doesn't fit my plans."

They drove in silence for the next couple of miles while Grace's thoughts churned. Finally she said, "I wish I had your faith, Kip. Or maybe your patience. Because I have a really hard time sitting back and waiting when it seems like God's falling down on the job."

"You think you're smarter than He is, do you?" Kip harrumphed.

"No. I mean—" Grace skewed her lips. "I mean if God won't do something, maybe we need to use some initiative, take matters into our own hands."

Kip cut her a sideways glance. "Don't go there, Grace. It'd only be asking for trouble."

Trouble? Seemed the people Grace cared most about had plenty of trouble to go around already. And she wasn't willing to stand by and watch things grow worse.

Ryan had just turned Christina over to her sidewalker volunteer Tuesday evening when his cell phone rang. The caller ID registered a number but no name, and that alone was enough to twist Ryan's gut. Yesterday he'd heard from a social worker wanting to set up a court-ordered home visitation. Guess the Burches weren't wasting any time pressing this custody suit.

Marching out of the arena, Ryan took the call, his jaw clenched as he muttered a terse hello.

"Hey, Ryan, it's Joe Wagner."

At the sound of his client's friendly voice, Ryan's tension melted. "Yes, sir, how can I help you?"

"That new shoe you put on Thaddeus a couple weeks ago is coming loose. Any chance you could come back by tomorrow?"

Ryan's toes throbbed at the mere mention of the Percheron's name. "I'll check my schedule. Can I call you back in an hour or so? I'm at Christina's riding class."

"Sounds fine. How's that little cutie doing? She sure knows her horses!"

"That she does." Ryan didn't feel like detailing his current worries. With a friendly good-bye, he snapped the phone onto his belt clip.

In the arena, Grace guided Christina's horse in a figure-eight pattern. Grace may be holding the lead rope, but Christina was doing a pretty good job of reining.

Ryan sighed. His little girl might be the world's youngest equine expert, but she still didn't get this whole "Mommy's in heaven" thing. Every few days she'd plop down in front of Ryan's laptop and remind him to get ready for Mommy's Skype call.

As Ryan started back to the arena, he saw Kip exit the barn. Kip waved him over. "Talk to Stan Turner yet?"

"Had an appointment first thing this morning." Which worked out well because Mrs. Airhart was free to watch Christina for a bit. "He's…cautiously optimistic."

"That's good."

"There's just one thing." Ryan explained about the social worker. "Stan thinks I shouldn't take Christina on my farrier rounds with me until this blows over."

Kip rocked on his boot heels. "He's got a point. Horse barns aren't exactly kid proof."

"Yeah, but what am I going to do with her? I'm *not* putting her back in day care."

"What about your neighbor lady?"

"Mrs. Airhart? She doesn't mind helping from time to time, but she's got a life. No way I could ask her to watch Christina thirty or forty hours a week." Ryan clenched his jaw. "I'm a good dad, Kip. I've never once put Christina in danger."

"I know that, and you know that. But if you want to keep her, looks like you're gonna have to convince a judge."

While Kip went on about his business, Ryan ambled into the arena and took his seat on the bleachers. A couple of the other dads tried to engage him in casual conversation, but he had a hard time feigning interest. Kip was right. If the Burches didn't drop this custody suit, Ryan would have to prove himself a model parent in every way.

Then, as he watched his daughter's riding lesson, his gaze shifted from Christina to Grace, and it suddenly felt as if he saw her with new eyes. She'd always been pretty, from her long, curly, strawberry-blond hair to the feminine curve of her hips. She led Belle around the arena with confidence, a sure but gentle hand on the lead rope...just like the hold she'd always had on Ryan's heart.

All these years and he'd never told her how he felt, never dared to breach the friendship barrier they'd so carefully erected. For one thing, he'd been too busy being a dad, not to mention too hung up on staying loyal to Shana and clinging to the impossible dream of forming a family with the mother of his child.

And Grace... The hours she put in at school and Cross Roads Farm, plus working part-time at the Kingsley Community Clinic, left little time for a social life. As a high school senior she'd set her sights on that occupational therapy degree, and nothing was going to stand in her way.

Grace's determination was only one of many traits Ryan admired about her. She was fun to be with, easy to talk to. She was caring and compassionate, a devoted sister, a loyal friend.

She was everything Ryan had ever wanted in a woman… in a wife. Watching her now—her easy walk, her hand's calming stroke along Belle's neck, her encouraging smiles as she glanced over her shoulder at Christina—he could hardly catch his breath. Why had he waited all these years, denying himself the love he could have had, when Grace had been standing right in front of him all along?

As the class ended, Grace led Belle to the dismounting area. While Sheridan and the sidewalker helped Christina down from the horse, Grace glanced toward the bleachers. Catching Ryan's eye, she tossed him a smile.

He grinned back. Kind of a silly, moonstruck grin, if she had to describe it. Must be exhaustion catching up with him. Heaven knew the poor guy had his hands full lately. Grace couldn't help wondering where things stood with the custody suit.

The thought soured her stomach, and she grew angry all over again that the Burches could be so callous.

Ryan ambled over to get Christina, and Grace tamped down her bitter feelings. She needed to be positive for Ryan's sake, because in the weeks ahead he'd need all the support he could get.

Except…he was still wearing that funny smile. "Hey, squirt."

Grace arched a brow. "Hey, scuzzy."

"Mind if Christina and I walk Belle to the barn with you?"

"Be my guest." Grace started toward the arena gate. This was unusual. Normally by the end of class Ryan hurried to get his tired little girl home, bathed, and tucked into bed.

Ryan propped Christina on his hip and watched from

outside Belle's stall as Grace unsaddled the horse and brushed her down. Each time Grace glanced up at them, she had the feeling Ryan wanted to say something, but then he'd look away or murmur something to Christina.

Leaving Belle's stall, Grace carried the saddle into the tack room. She found Ryan waiting for her outside the door, and the image that flitted through her mind was that of a hungry puppy waiting for a handout. Something was definitely up with the guy.

By now Christina was yawning wider than the Grand Canyon, her head bobbing against Ryan's shoulder.

Grace smoothed Christina's silky hair. "You should get this sweet girl home to bed."

"Yeah, but I, uh…" He moved out of the way as another horse leader hauled gear into the tack room. "See, I…"

Folding her arms, Grace narrowed her eyes. "Just spit it out, Ry. You've been *not* saying something ever since we left the arena, and it's making me nervous."

He drew a long, slow breath through his nose then blew it out in a huff. "Grace, would you have dinner with me tomorrow night?"

Okay, *that* came out of left field. And he'd used the word *dinner*, as opposed to the more casual-sounding *supper*. Grace's glance darted every which way while she formed a reply. "I get the feeling you're not talking pizza or Chinese takeout."

"Yeah. I mean, no." Ryan's mouth twitched. "I thought we'd go get a steak, somewhere quiet where we could talk."

"What about Christina?"

"I phoned Mrs. Airhart a few minutes ago. She said she can stay with her."

He'd already asked his neighbor to babysit? This sounded suspiciously like a date, and Grace wasn't sure how she felt about that. "I don't know, Ryan. On Wednesdays I don't usually get home from UNC until after six. Why don't I just meet you in town? We could grab a burger—"

"Please, Grace." Christina squirmed, and Ryan snuggled her closer against his side. "I know it's short notice, but I really want to take you out."

As the sun set beyond the arena, one golden-pink ray pierced the tree line and lit Ryan's face. Quiet desperation shone in his eyes, a look that seared Grace's heart. "Okay," she said, against all her better judgment. "I'll be ready by six thirty."

Chapter 9

By Wednesday afternoon Grace's nerves were so frayed that she almost called Ryan to cancel. What was up with him anyway, pulling this relational switcheroo on her without warning?

Shana's death and the Burches' custody suit must be turning him into a basket case. That was the only explanation that made sense.

Munching on a granola bar while she studied between classes, Grace caught the muffled chime from her cell phone indicating a text message. She reached across the table for her shoulder bag and fished out the phone.

Great. Her advisor wanted a conference. Today.

She checked the time. Thirty minutes yet until her next class began. Might as well go right now. Maybe Mrs. Lieber had an update about the occupational therapy program.

Five minutes later, Grace tapped on Mrs. Lieber's door. "You wanted to see me, ma'am?"

"Come in, Miss Lorimer." The woman's stiff smile didn't bode well. She motioned Grace into a chair while she thumbed through a stack of papers. When she found what she was looking for, she laced her fingers atop the page and shook her head. "I've grown concerned about your grades this semester. You do understand the occupational therapy program accepts a limited number of applicants *and* only the *most* qualified students?"

"Yes, ma'am." Grace tasted stomach acid at the back of her throat. "I've had some personal concerns lately. I'll work harder, I promise."

The advisor's expression softened. "You're an excellent student, Grace, and I know you're having to put yourself through school with very little help from family or scholarships. I also understand how daunting the prospect of paying off student loans can be. But in the long run, you could be doing yourself a favor by cutting back on your part-time work hours and applying for additional loan money so you can focus more fully on your studies."

Rising, Grace shifted her books to one hip. "Thank you. I'll think about it."

As Grace plodded across campus to her next class, she decided one sure way to cut back on distractions was to nip this "date" thing with Ryan in the bud. She set her books down on a bench and found his number in her speed dial. "Ryan? It's Grace. I'm sorry, but I need—"

"Can I call you back?" He sounded edgy. "I'm kind of in the middle of something."

"Oh. Are you working?"

"No, I'm at home." Static filled Grace's ear as Ryan exhaled sharply. "Grace, I have to go. I'll explain later when I pick you up." The line went dead.

Dumbfounded, Grace stared at the phone in her hand. So much for breaking her date…if that's what it was. She'd have to go through with it now but just this once. She'd make sure Ryan understood she'd always be there for him, but their relationship could never be anything but friendship.

With effort she managed to push Ryan from her mind and make it through her next class without losing focus. But on the drive home to Cross Roads Farm her hands grew clammy on the steering wheel as she mentally rehearsed several variations of the speech she planned to recite over dinner.

Dinner. How could one tiny, two-syllable word turn Grace's life totally upside down?

Flinging her purse and books on the sofa, Grace raced to the bedroom. She kicked off her sneakers while thumbing through her closet in search of something a little nicer than jeans and the pullover top she'd been wearing all day. Something nice enough for *dinner* at a steak house.

With Ryan.

Who would arrive in less than fifteen minutes!

The butterflies dive-bombing each other in Grace's stomach made no sense. No sense at all.

She'd barely brushed the tangles out of her hair when a knock sounded on her front door. With a steadying breath she straightened the blue silk blouse she'd changed into, slipped her feet into a pair of black flats, and marched to the door.

"Hey, squ—" Reddening, Ryan cleared his throat. "Hi, Grace. Am I too early?"

He looked dapper in a gray plaid shirt, black jeans, and boots polished to perfection. Self-consciously Grace tucked a strand of hair behind her ear. "I just need to get a sweater."

When she returned from the closet, Ryan helped her drape the sweater around her shoulders. The subtle scent of his aftershave, citrus with a hint of spice, brought a pleasant tickle to her nose.

"Sorry I couldn't talk earlier," Ryan said. A subtle grimace creased his left cheek. "The social worker decided to show up unannounced."

Grace angled him a confused look as she locked the cottage door on their way out. "You were at home all afternoon? What about your work?"

"I'm cutting back on my appointments until I figure out what to do with Christina." He explained briefly about Stan Turner's recommendation.

"I'm sorry, Ryan. That's got to be hard on both of you." Grace reached for the passenger door handle only to find Ryan had grabbed it first. She thrust her hand to her side and tried to breathe normally while he opened the door.

So this was what first-date jitters felt like. Unable to think of a single thing to say, Grace faced forward as Ryan drove toward town, her hands clasped tightly in her lap. Ryan's frequent sighs, combined with his death grip on the steering wheel, suggested he felt equally uncomfortable.

Well, it was his own fault for using the *dinner* word.

"Can I ask where we're going?" Grace finally asked. She'd figured out two turns back that they weren't dining in Kingsley.

"Thought we'd try this new steak place I heard of over in Matthews. I made a reservation for seven fifteen." He nodded toward the dashboard clock. "We should be right on time."

Grace couldn't remember the last time she ate somewhere that required reservations. Another glance toward Ryan and her insides felt like melting wax. Had she never noticed before how handsome he was? As a starry-eyed teen she'd thought him bad-boy cute. But Ryan the man was something else entirely. Tough and tender, serious yet fun-loving, he'd matured into someone Grace both admired and respected.

Someone she cared for deeply.

And that scared her half out of her wits.

"Reservation for O'Keefe?" Ryan dared to rest his hand on the small of Grace's back as he waited for the restaurant hostess to find his name. He liked the slick feel of Grace's blouse against his palm. He liked that she'd left her hair down and the way it spiraled across her shoulders like a shimmering, golden waterfall.

"This way, please." The hostess gathered menus and led them through the softly lit dining area. Stopping at one of the alcoves, she whisked a lighter from her pocket and touched the flame to a candle. "Your server will be right with you."

"Wow, this is fancy." Grace shot him an uneasy smile as he pulled out her chair.

"Not exactly burgers and shakes at Cook-Out, is it?" Ryan jostled the table as he took the seat across from her. Great. Might as well announce to the world how nervous he was.

A tall, thin server in a white shirt, black pants, and black brocade vest sauntered into the alcove. "Good evening. My name is Ivan. May I bring you something from the bar?"

Ryan peered questioningly at Grace over the top of his menu.

She gave her head a small shake. "Just water, please. With lemon."

"Same here." Ryan turned his attention to the menu. A glance at the prices made him wince. He could buy his own steak and cook it on the backyard grill for a whole lot less. Ambience definitely came with a price.

But Grace was worth every penny.

They didn't talk much during dinner. Didn't eat much either. Ryan kept mentally rehearsing what he'd planned to ask Grace this evening, while praying she'd be receptive to the idea.

The next time Ivan came by to check on them, he looked askance at their plates. "If anything wasn't prepared to your liking…"

"Oh, no," Grace protested. "Everything was delicious." Glancing at Ryan, she pulled her lower lip between her teeth. "Guess I wasn't very hungry."

"Me neither." Ryan laid his knife and fork across his plate. "Maybe we could have a couple takeout containers… and how about two decafs?"

Ivan returned shortly with the coffee and boxed up their leftovers. After the server left them, Ryan cleared his throat as he stirred cream into his mug. He glanced across the table, nervously meeting Grace's gaze. "I'm sorry if this evening's been awkward for you. I just wanted it to be special."

"It has been." Grace averted her eyes while she sipped her decaf. She set down the mug and looked straight at Ryan. "I guess I'm wondering why, though. I mean…"

"Yeah." Every nerve tingling, Ryan braced his arms along the edge of the table. He had to get this right, had to make her understand he wasn't asking only because of Christina or the custody suit. But he also didn't want to send her screaming into the next county with his sudden declaration of love.

Because that's what it was…*love.* A word he felt certain Grace wasn't ready to hear.

"Grace, I want—*need*—you to think about something. And please don't answer till you've heard me out, okay?"

She hugged herself. "You're scaring me, Ryan."

She was scared? He was half out of his mind with the

fear that she'd reject him flat out, never give him, or herself, a chance. "Grace, you know I care for you. Always have since the first day we met."

Her shoulders relaxed slightly. A tiny smile turned up the corners of her mouth. "Even when my overprotective big brother threatened to hog-tie you and toss you in the manure bin if you even *looked* cross-eyed at me?"

"That is one time I have to say Kip did *not* mince words." Ryan's face warmed. One hand crept across the table toward Grace. "But I'd have risked even the manure bin for one of your smiles. Still would."

It seemed forever before she huffed a quiet sigh and extended her own hand to meet Ryan's. Her cool fingertips curled into his palm and brought an ache to his heart. "Oh, Ryan," she said, her voice soft but firm, "please don't do this. Don't spoil a perfectly wonderful friendship."

"I don't want that either. I hope we'll always be friends." He stroked the side of her hand with his thumb. "But what I'm about to ask you…well, it's gonna sound crazy, and it probably is."

"Ryan—"

He cut her off with a raised palm. Time to spit it out, lay his cards on the table, say the words he'd been practicing in his head all evening. "Grace, I want you to marry me."

Grace yanked her hand into her lap. What she really wanted to do was give herself a good, hard head slap, because she could not *possibly* have heard Ryan correctly.

Marry him?

"I know this is hitting you out of left field." Ryan extended both his hands across the table, palms up in a pleading gesture. "But it could be a good thing for both of us."

Twisting her napkin, Grace glanced toward the main dining room, hoping the sound of their voices didn't carry beyond the alcove. Her face must be tomato red by now, and the last thing she needed was an audience. She closed her eyes briefly, realization dawning. "Is this about the custody suit?"

"I admit that's what got me thinking about…us. But it's not the only thing. I meant what I said, Grace. I…I care for you." His throat worked. He lowered his head. "Very much."

With a whispery sigh she slid her hands into his. "I care about you, too, Ry. And you know I'd do anything to help you keep Christina. But marriage? You're right. It's crazy." She shook her head. "And utterly impossible."

"Why? Just think about it, will you?" Ryan's tone hardened into a desperate plea. "Christina needs a mom, someone who'll be there for her when I'm not. And I need y—" He bit his lip and glanced away.

She couldn't let herself be swayed. "Ryan, listen to me. What you're asking is more than I can give. You know how much it means to me to finish school and get my OT certification. You know how hard I've worked for this." Withdrawing her hands, she tucked them beneath her arms. "I'm sorry, but being a wife…a mom…doesn't fit into my plans."

Ryan laced his fingers in the center of the table, squeezing so hard that his knuckles whitened. "I'm not asking you to give up your dream."

"Really? Because it sure sounds like it."

Glassware shook as Ryan's urgency intensified. He spread his fingers and rested his palms on the table. "I'm not rich by any means, but I make good money as a farrier. Married to me, you wouldn't have to work part-time anymore."

Cautiously she lifted her chin.

"See, I could adjust my work hours so that when you're at school, I'm home with Christina. When I'm out on calls, you and Christina can hang out together. Just set her up with a horse book, drawing paper, and pencils, and I promise, you'll have all the study time you need."

"Wow." Grace shook her head in stunned disbelief. "You've really thought this through."

"We could make it work, Grace. I know we could."

Her decaf had grown cold, but she sipped it anyway. Anything to stall for time. She couldn't believe she was actually considering this absurd idea. Peeking at Ryan over the rim of her mug, she saw the hope in his eyes... and something more. A tiny knot had formed between his brows. His lips were parted, curling up at the corners almost imperceptibly.

Just then Ivan appeared at their table with a coffee carafe. "May I freshen—"

"We're fine." Without even looking up, Ryan asked for the check, and the server quietly stepped away.

The interruption was enough to return Grace to her senses. Scooting her chair back, she drew her purse into her lap. "I'm going to the ladies' room now. When I come back, I'd like you to take me home. I have a lot of thinking to do."

At least she hadn't flat-out said no.

Yet.

But the evening wasn't over. And with neither of them talking, the drive back to Cross Roads Farm seemed like an eternity. Ryan prayed that Grace's silence meant she was giving his proposal serious consideration.

Proposal, right. He hadn't even offered her a ring. This was *not* how he imagined asking the girl of his dreams to marry him. And he hadn't even used the word *love*.

Oh, but he had wanted to. He'd had to bite his tongue more than once tonight for fear of scaring her worse than he already had. He knew Grace all too well. He knew how she held herself aloof, avoiding relationships, never letting any guy get too close.

He knew because, ever since Shana, he'd done exactly the same thing with women.

Thoughts of Shana returned him briefly to those years of vulnerability. Fresh out of high school, when he hoped to put his bad-boy image behind him and make something of his life, he'd needed someone like Shana—strong, independent, determined. She'd helped him believe what Kip had always told him, that he could be more than the product of lousy parenting. He could reach higher. Dream bigger. Go further.

Except Shana's independence was the very thing that finally came between them. She hadn't wanted to *need* anyone, not even when they'd found out they were having a baby. So when Shana told Ryan she wouldn't marry him, he'd decided it was best not to need anyone either. Love hurt, so why put your heart on the line?

Then Christina came along, and Ryan discovered a whole different kind of love. The unconditional kind. The kind that endures through heartache and happiness, feast and famine, good times and bad. How long had he prayed that someday Shana would discover her need for that kind of love as well? How long had he waited for her to come to her senses, to become his wife and stand by his side as they faced life together?

He was no longer sure exactly when he'd subconsciously replaced Shana with Grace in that picture. It could have been weeks or months. It could have been years. He sensed only that Grace had been tucked away in his heart all along, and that maybe…maybe God had been preparing them both for this moment. Now he could only pray that Grace would finally let down her guard and allow Ryan into her heart.

A misty halo surrounded the mercury-vapor light over

the barn as Ryan parked beside Grace's cottage. After shutting off the engine, he reached across the console and touched Grace's arm, a silent signal she should wait for him to come around and get her door.

Stepping from the cab, she let him take her hand but kept her eyes lowered. "Thanks for dinner." She nodded toward the takeout box she carried, offering Ryan a quick glance and a wry smile. "And tomorrow's lunch."

Joking with him—that had to be a good sign, right? Ryan walked her to the door and held the box while she rummaged for her key. Before she stepped inside, he caught her wrist. "Grace."

"Please, Ryan. I need some time."

His breathing grew shallow and quick. His heart thumped so hard it felt like an earthquake in his chest. "Just let me…"

He set the takeout container on the window box and slid his arm around her waist, drawing her close. A delicate floral scent filled his senses as his fingers got lost in her hair. Before he could even reason out why he shouldn't do this, much less stop himself before it was too late, he lowered his lips upon hers. She tasted sweet, with a hint of minty chocolate from the after-dinner candies their server had brought with the check.

While her mouth melted into the kiss, her hands crept up between them and pressed against Ryan's chest in a weak and futile attempt to ward off this invasion. He was taking advantage, and he knew it, but he was powerless to stop.

Powerless to stop. Exactly how he and Shana had become parents before either of them was ready.

Sanity returning, Ryan gently released his hold and stepped back. He handed Grace her takeout box. "It's late. I'd better get home to Christina."

"Christina. Right." Grace sounded breathless, a little dazed. She brushed the backs of her fingers across her lips.

Ryan took two steps toward his pickup then halted. Thumbs hooked in his front pockets, he murmured, "I'll make you a good husband, Grace. I'll care for you like nobody else ever could."

"I know," she whispered, and then the door closed behind her.

Chapter 10

"Great riding today, kids." Grace perused the smiling faces of her five Saturday morning students. "Time to dismount and untack your horses."

She strolled down the row to make sure everyone followed safe procedures as the volunteers assisted their riders to the ground then helped them remove saddles and brush down their horses. After the horses had been led from the arena and the children had rejoined their parents, Grace reminded everyone there would be no classes next Saturday because of the annual barbecue cook-off fund-raiser.

When everyone had gone, Grace plopped onto a bleacher seat to make progress notes in her lesson folder. Hearing the clink of the arena gate latch, she looked up to see Sheridan striding over.

"Good class?" Sheridan plunked down beside Grace.

"Couldn't ask for better." Next to Melanie's name Grace wrote, *good reining, needs to work on posture.*

"Mom called this morning. She and Tom are loading up the RV and should be here sometime Wednesday."

Linda and Tom Jacobs brought a barbecue team all the way from Nacogdoches, Texas, every year for the big event. Grace hadn't seen Linda since Christmas, and she could hardly wait to sit down for a heart-to-heart with the woman who'd become more of a mom to Grace than the mother who raised her.

She jotted a few more notes before closing the folder. "I can't believe the cook-off is only a week away. I feel awful for not helping more."

"Don't sweat it. We've got a great volunteer committee this year." Sheridan bumped Grace's shoulder with her own. "Anyway, you've had plenty to keep you busy, what with work and school and everything else."

Being reminded of the *everything else* part made Grace's stomach clench. She hadn't told anyone yet about Ryan's marriage proposal. Hadn't even decided how to answer him, and she'd had ten days to think about it! Seeing him at church and then at Christina's riding class this week had been awkward, to say the least.

Grace pushed up from the bleachers. "Well, I'm making a point of freeing up my schedule for next weekend so you can put me to work wherever you need me."

Sheridan fell in beside her as they walked toward the arena gate then blocked her way as they started through. "Look, Grace, I don't mean to pry, but…you'd tell me if anything was bothering you, right?"

Hugging her lesson folder, Grace offered a twitchy smile. "What makes you think something's bothering me?"

"Mainly because you've kept so much to yourself lately. Kip and I hardly see you except for the riding classes." Sheridan lightly touched Grace's arm, her tone softening.

"You took such good care of me when I miscarried. I'd like to be there for you."

Releasing a shivery sigh, Grace leaned against the rail. "Oh, Sher, you don't know the half of it!"

Five minutes later they sat at Sheridan's kitchen table sipping sweet tea while Grace poured out first her shock and then her ambivalence about Ryan's proposal. "Part of me sees the logic in what he's suggesting. If Christina had a stable, two-parent home, the courts would have a really hard time taking her away from her dad. And I can't deny how much easier my life would be if I weren't dividing my time between school and work."

With a sad smile, Sheridan folded her arms along the table edge. "Honey, marriage isn't about logic. It's about *love*."

Grace closed her eyes, remembering the kiss that had shaken her to her core. Her voice trembled when she said, "I'm pretty sure Ryan's in love with me."

"And?" Sheridan leaned closer, one eyebrow arched in a knowing expression.

"And…I care a lot for him." Grace shifted sideways, unable to meet Sheridan's gaze.

"But if you don't return his feelings—"

The back door swung open, and Kip trudged in wearing a scowl. He whipped off his Stetson and tossed it on the rack beside the door before crumpling into the nearest chair.

Sheridan rose and poured another glass of tea. "What's got you so upset, hon?"

"Just disgusted with the headaches this custody business is givin' Ryan." Kip harrumphed as he bent forward to pull off his boots.

Sharing a look with Grace, Sheridan asked, "You talked to him?"

"Got off the phone a few minutes ago." Kip took a long

swig of tea. "He's fit to be tied trying to keep his customers happy while making sure he has someone to look after
Christina. His neighbor lady's helped him out several times,
but now her sister's having surgery and she's flying to Fort
Wayne this afternoon. She'll be gone at least two weeks."

Grace fought against the tightness in her chest as she
tried to draw a breath. Her arms felt weak and shaky as she
pushed up from the table. "Is Ryan at home now?"

"Said he was."

Sheridan caught Grace's arm before she could bolt for
the door. "What are you planning to do?"

"Something I should have done days ago." With a help-
less shrug and an ache in her heart, she pleaded with her
eyes for her sister-in-law's understanding before turning
to leave.

"Don't be reckless, Grace." Sheridan darted after her.
"You haven't thought this through."

"There's no more time for thinking. I won't let them take
Christina away."

Ignoring Sheridan's pleas and her brother's confused
stare, Grace plunged through the door. Moments later, she'd
grabbed her purse and keys and was speeding toward Kingsley.

"Joy needs to be brushed." Christina tugged on the seam
of Ryan's jeans as he set their lunchtime soup bowls in the
dishwasher. "She has a tangle in her tail."

"One tangle isn't gonna hurt her till I finish the dishes."
He glanced down to see two beady little Pomeranian eyes
peering up expectantly. The pint-size ball of fur sure had
a monster-size hold on Christina's heart, not a bad thing
these days when everything else in their lives was in utter
turmoil.

He'd been reluctant at first when Mrs. Airhart asked if

Ryan would look after Joy while she was away. But Christina had jumped right into the conversation with enough doggy facts to fill an encyclopedia, which, in Aspie language, meant she really, *really* wanted Joy to stay with them.

"Mrs. Airhart put the measuring cup for Joy's food in the canister. Joy gets exactly one-half cup in the morning and one-half cup at suppertime." Christina bent down to stroke the dog's fluffy coat. "And plenty of fresh water all day long."

Ryan closed the dishwasher. "Yes, punkin, it's all written down on the instructions Mrs. A left us. And I'm putting you in charge of checking Joy's water bowl, okay? Whenever it gets low, come and tell me and I'll—"

The doorbell chimed, sending Ryan's stomach plummeting to his toes. If he had one more surprise visit from that social worker, he was liable to do something drastic. Like maybe whisk Christina away to Brazil and disappear forever. They had horses to shoe in Brazil, didn't they?

With Joy yapping at his heels, he marched to the front door then grabbed the little dog and tucked her under his arm. Just let that sassy social worker say something about a dog in the house, and he'd slam the door in her face.

Hand on the knob, he squared his shoulders and strove for his most convincing "perfect daddy" veneer—only to exchange it for a major case of nervous stomach when he pulled open the door and saw Grace standing on his porch.

Fingertips tucked in her jeans pockets, she hiked her chin. "Hey, scuzzy."

Ryan swallowed. "Hey, squirt."

They both stood there like shy schoolkids for a full minute, looking everywhere but at each other. Then Grace said, "You have a dog now?"

"No, this is Joy. We're keeping her for Mrs. Airhart."
Absently, Ryan scratched the dog behind her pointy ears.

Grace extended one hand toward the dog, who licked
Grace's fingers with her darting pink tongue. "I heard your
neighbor left to be with her sister. That's why I'm here, actually." Peering around Ryan, she asked, "Can I come in?
We need to talk."

Ryan glanced over his shoulder and saw Christina me-
ticulously laying out Joy's leash, comb, brush, and chew
toys along the sofa cushions. Whatever Grace had come to
say, he didn't need his daughter overhearing. Setting Joy
down, he shooed her toward Christina. Then he stepped
onto the porch and pulled the door partly closed. Heat rose
in his neck as he stared at his boot tips. "It'd been so long,
I figured you'd decided never to speak to me again."

"What did you expect, Ryan? After what you laid on me
at dinner that night, and then kissing me like you did—I've
never been so rattled and confused in my life."

"If I could take it all back, I would. Because the last thing
I ever wanted to do was ruin our friendship."

"Well, you can't take it back, and anyway—" Grace suddenly flung her hands skyward, a frustrated growl tearing
from her throat. "Just let me say what I came to say, okay?
I've thought it over and…I'll marry you."

The words tore through Ryan like a knife thrust. He
was pretty sure his heart stopped beating for a moment.
"Grace, I—"

"Hold on. I'm not through." She folded her arms and
paced back and forth on the small porch. "I'll try my best
to be a good mom for Christina and a good wife for you—
except for the part that involves the bedroom. I'm not ready
for that, and I don't know if I ever will be."

"I understand." He tried to stand there calmly when his

arms ached to hold her, and all he wanted to do was kiss away this fear she had of letting herself love him.

Gripping the porch rail, she swiveled her head and nailed him with a steely glare. "I need your word, Ryan O'Keefe. Promise me you won't push for more."

Though it sapped him of every last ounce of strength and no small measure of hope, he lifted his right hand, palm outward. "Strictly platonic. You have my word."

"Okay." Her gaze softened, but only slightly, as it shifted toward the azaleas beneath the front windows. "How soon do you want to do this?"

How about right now? he wanted to shout, still in shock that she'd actually agreed. Maybe not for the reasons he'd longed for, but… *Dear Lord, help her open her heart and let me in.*

He forced himself to think in practical terms. "First thing's a license, I guess, which we can't get until Monday at the earliest. I'll phone Pastor Wolfe and see when he could perform the ceremony."

With a tense sigh, Grace swung around and braced her hips against the porch rail. "I didn't think about needing to talk to the pastor."

"That bothers you?" Now Ryan felt uneasy. He'd be married in the church or not at all.

She stared out toward the street. "It just…makes it more real."

"It *is* real, Grace. You'll be my wife in the eyes of God, and I wouldn't have it any other way." Daring to step closer, he took her by the shoulders and gazed hard into eyes that looked back at him like a frightened doe. "I'll honor my promise—have no fear of that. But I want you to know from day one that this marriage isn't only about Christina or the custody suit. I asked *you* to marry me, Grace. I asked you because there's no one else in God's whole creation I could ever see myself married to. I asked you because I'm in love with you and have been for a long, long time."

Hands folded between his knees, Pastor Wolfe leaned toward Grace. "Do you love him?"

It was just the two of them now, chatting in the pastor's cluttered office following Sunday morning worship. Floor-to-ceiling shelves groaned beneath the weight of more Bibles, commentaries, and other theological books than Grace could count. Her gaze skimmed the titles as if one would pop out and provide whatever answer would convince Pastor Wolfe to marry her and Ryan.

"Of course I love Ryan," she finally said, her tone more defensive than she'd intended. She loved him as a friend, certainly. Could God strike you down for answering a pastor with something less than the whole truth?

"I'm only asking because this is so sudden. I'm concerned you and Ryan may not have thoroughly evaluated your reasons for getting married right away." Pastor Wolfe leaned back in his chair. "I can understand his wanting to provide a secure family situation for Christina. But before I agree to officiate, I need to know this will be a home created out of love, not desperation."

Tears unexpectedly rose in Grace's eyes. "Can't it be both, Pastor? Love *and* desperation? Because Ryan's desperate to keep Christina, and I'm desperate to help him. He's the best father in the world, and I won't see his daughter taken from him."

Pastor Wolfe dipped his chin and exhaled thoughtfully. "What else is going on here, Grace? Does this have anything to do with the fact that your brother and Sheridan haven't been able to become parents?"

His words cut deep, revealing a truth Grace hadn't

wanted to face. She knotted her fists, throat closing until she could barely speak. "I'm not letting God win this one."

"We're not at war with God." Pastor Wolfe shook his head sadly. "Jesus came to bring us peace with our heavenly Father, not punishment and condemnation. But as long as we're living in a fallen world, bad things will happen to good people. Good people like your brother. Good people like Ryan." He inclined his head toward her, his mouth softening into a knowing smile. "Good people like you."

Instantly Grace recalled her mother's selfishness and deception—all the wasted years of growing up without a father, never knowing about her brother, missing out on so much love. The memories fueled her determination to help Ryan keep his daughter.

She turned pleading eyes upon the pastor. "It'll destroy Ryan if the Burches get Christina. They'll do everything they can to keep them apart. You know they will."

Pastor Wolfe lowered his head in silent agreement. After several moments he nodded thoughtfully. "All right, Grace, if you can assure me that you and Ryan are entering into marriage with every intention of honoring this covenant according to God's plan, then I'll agree to perform the ceremony."

Three days later, Grace sat before the mirror in the church's bride room while Linda Cross Jacobs plaited white ribbons and tiny blue silk flowers into her hair.

Linda beamed a smile at Grace's reflection. "You look beautiful, honey. Ryan is one lucky young man."

Shortly after Linda and Tom had arrived at the farm that afternoon, Grace had taken Linda aside to explain the reasons for this spur-of-the-moment wedding. She'd also confessed the stipulations she'd placed upon Ryan that this would be a marriage in name only. Now, releasing a shivery breath, she asked, "Do you still think I'm doing the right thing?"

"I think what you're doing is selfless and admirable." After tying a bow at the bottom of Grace's braid, Linda scooted next to her on the narrow bench and tucked her arm around Grace's waist. "I also believe it won't be long before you discover your feelings for Ryan go much, much deeper than friendship. Trust yourself, Grace. Trust your heart."

Unfortunately, Grace's heart was the one thing she trusted least.

A knock sounded on the door, and Sheridan peeked in. "Grace, are you ready?"

Grace's stomach heaved, making her grateful she'd skipped lunch. Though she doubted God heard, she prayed anyway. *Help me, Lord! Help this be right for all of us.*

Then, standing, she smoothed the skirt of the plain white cotton dress she'd found at Kingsley Mercantile yesterday during a last-minute shopping trip. With a bracing breath, she turned toward Sheridan and smiled with more confidence than she felt. "Ready as I'll ever be."

The ceremony would be a simple one, with only the family in attendance. And really, that was all Grace needed or wanted. Nathan and Filipa had provided a floral arrangement for the altar and a bouquet of fragrant spring flowers for Grace. Ryan had asked Kip to stand up with him, and Grace had asked Sheridan. Kip would also walk Grace down the aisle.

He met her at the entrance to the sanctuary and offered his arm. "Lookin' pretty as a summer day," he said, kissing her lightly on the cheek.

"Oh, Kip—" She sniffed back a tear. If she lived a thousand years, she'd never be able to express to her brother how much he meant to her.

"Now, now, none of that." He looked her up and down.

"You got all that bride stuff you're supposed to have? Somethin' borrowed, somethin' blue?"

His teasing made her laugh. "Sheridan let me borrow her pearl earrings. Linda wove blue flowers into my hair."

Kip rummaged around in the pocket of his western-style suit coat. Bringing out his closed fist, he said, "Then there's just one more thing—a lucky penny for your shoe." He opened his hand to reveal a shiny new penny. "See, it was minted the year you and I found each other, the same year you and Ryan first met. Not sayin' I believe in luck, but I figure God blessed all of us that year, so it's worth remembering today."

Grace fought back tears while Kip knelt to slip the penny into her shoe. She'd never expected to be so emotional today, never expected to be so nervous about an event that in truth was only a formality. Or at least that's how she chose to see it. One friend helping another. Nothing more, nothing less.

But when she stepped through the church doors and saw Ryan beaming at her from the chancel steps, she knew exactly why this wedding frightened her so. No one but Ryan O'Keefe had ever made her tingle at his touch or caused her heart to flutter with just a glance. No one but Ryan could make her question everything she'd ever believed about the futility of falling in love.

Chapter 11

There wouldn't be a honeymoon, which, because of Christina, Ryan didn't have too much trouble explaining to his friends at the wedding. They all sympathized, of course, having no idea about his private agreement with Grace.

Although he suspected Linda Jacobs might be aware of the arrangement, because when Ryan's mother offered to stay in town an extra night or two and keep Christina, Linda had come to his rescue with the reminder that Ryan was also taking care of his neighbor's dog for a couple of weeks. Though Ryan and his mom had been getting along well the last few years, one thing they didn't share was an affinity for animals.

Following a family dinner in one of Kingsley Station's private dining rooms, Ryan and Grace said their good-byes, gathered up Christina, and headed out to the pickup. Someone—probably Kip and Nathan—had soaped the windows with *Just Married* and several huge hearts with arrows through them. Balloons and tin cans had been tied to the bumper.

Already overwhelmed and no doubt very confused, Christina jogged on her toes as she gripped Ryan's hand. "It's all messy! How will you clean it up, Daddy?"

"Not to worry, sugarplum. I'll take the truck through a car wash first thing in the morning." As he opened the rear door for Christina, he glanced at Grace, who had already climbed into the passenger seat. A big white heart framed her face as she turned toward him, and he shot her a reassuring smile.

The clatter of tin cans followed them all the way home, much to Christina's annoyance. She kept twisting around to look out the back window. Ryan had worked for days to prepare her for the wedding, but he still wasn't sure she understood. Explaining what would happen at the ceremony had been complicated enough. The really hard part, though, was helping her grasp the idea that Grace would now be part of their family. He was careful not to use the words *new mommy*, hoping that, in time, Christina would come to that realization on her own.

Grace had already moved some of her things over earlier in the week, so tonight she'd brought only a small travel bag. Ryan set it on the back porch while he unlocked the door and then had to snatch up Joy before she licked them all to death with her over-the-top doggy greeting.

Christina raced past them into the house, dancing on her toes and flapping her hands. "Daddy, I'm hungry! Daddy, I'm hungry!"

A yippy dog, an out-of-control kid… The tension of the day caught up with Ryan, and he just about lost it. He tossed Grace's travel bag onto the sofa. "Christina, that's enough! You already had dinner at the restaurant, not to mention way too much cake. Now you need to put your pajamas on and go to bed."

"No! I'm still hungry, and I want a bedtime snack."

Grace scooped Christina into her arms, holding her firmly against her chest and rubbing the little girl's back. "It's okay, sweetie. I'll fix you something. Do you like cinnamon toast?"

Christina sniffled and relaxed slightly. "I like it with chocolate milk."

"Good. Then I'd like you to sit quietly while I fix it. Can you do that?"

When Christina nodded, Grace put her down, and she crawled into a chair at the kitchen table.

Staring in both gratitude and amazement, Ryan realized he still clutched the little Pomeranian under his arm. He angled his head toward the back door. "I'm gonna take Joy out for a short walk."

By the time he returned, the house was quiet, a faint aroma of cinnamon toast lingering in the air. He found Grace in Christina's room. Christina was in her pajamas, snuggled next to Grace in the bed as Grace read aloud about the wild ponies of Chincoteague.

The sight of his girls—*his girls!*—looking content and happy gripped his heart so fiercely that he had to bite his lip to keep from crying. This was the family he'd always dreamed of, the family he'd begun to doubt he'd ever have.

Only one thing could make tonight even better, but it was the one thing Ryan didn't dare hope for.

Finishing the page she was reading, Grace caught his eye, and her lips quirked in a half smile. She slipped off the bed and laid Christina's book on the nightstand. "Okay, sweetie, time for lights out. Here's your dad to tuck you in."

Grace's hand brushed Ryan's as she stepped past him. Her braid had come loose, the tails of a slender white ribbon trailing down her back. It took all of Ryan's willpower not to pull her into his arms and let his fingers get lost in those thick, strawberry-blond curls. Instead, he strode into the room and brushed aside Christina's shaggy bangs as he bent to kiss her good night. "I love you, punkin. Sweet dreams."

Christina rose up on one elbow. "Where's Joy? Joy needs to go to bed, too."

"Oh, yeah, how could I forget?" From the first night Mrs. Airhart had brought Joy over, Christina had insisted on taking the little dog to bed with her. Ryan looked down to see the dog waiting patiently at his feet, her tiny pink tongue darting in and out. He lifted Joy onto the bed. "All righty, pup, here you go."

Curling her arms around the fuzzy Pomeranian, Christina squinted up at Ryan. "Joy is sleeping with me. Is Grace going to sleep with you?"

The question hit Ryan where it hurt. "Uh, no, sweetie. Daddy's gonna sleep on the sofa for now."

Grace heard the disappointment in Ryan's voice and wished she hadn't been the cause of it.

She also wished he'd agreed to sleep in his own bed and given her the sofa. She was, after all, the one who'd stipulated separate sleeping arrangements. Unfortunately, in a house this small there weren't many options. Maybe soon they could find a three-bedroom rental somewhere. In the meantime, they'd have to make do.

She'd just finished cleaning up the remnants of Christina's cinnamon toast snack when Ryan ambled into the kitchen. "Need anything?" she asked. "I could make us some toast and milk."

"Actually, that sounds pretty good." Ryan took two glasses from the cupboard. "I'll pour the milk if you'll do your magic with the cinnamon toast. Christina just informed me you make it way better than I do."

A few minutes later they sat at the table munching whole-wheat toast spread with butter and sprinkled generously with sugar and cinnamon. Ryan groaned appreciatively. "Yep, Christina was right."

"I'm glad you approve." Grace took another bite of toast but had to work it down over the tightness in her throat. "At least cooking for you is one 'wifely duty' I can fulfill."

"Grace...don't." Ryan snaked his hand across the table to capture hers. "I understand. I really do."

"Are you sure?" She dared a glance into his dusky, gray-green eyes and wished she hadn't, for all the pain she saw there.

"We talked all this through, remember? I've told you how I feel about you, but I'll never pressure you for more than you're willing to give."

"Thank you." The words came out on a whispered breath.

Squeezing her hand, Ryan tipped his head toward Christina's room. "I'm the one who needs to thank you. If you hadn't stepped in with Christina like you did, no telling how this evening might have turned out."

"She just got overexcited with all the wedding hullaba-loo." Grace chuckled. "Those three servings of cake probably didn't help."

"That little girl does love her carbs." Sitting back, Ryan finished his toast and washed it down with a long gulp of milk. "Sure was nice of Sheridan and Filipa to arrange the reception. I wasn't expecting that."

"Me, neither." Sparkling punch, a sheet cake decorated with white roses, and dainty white cocktail napkins imprinted with *Grace & Ryan* and today's date—simple but memorable. As if Grace could ever forget the day she became Mrs. Ryan O'Keefe.

She glanced across the table at her husband—her *husband*!—and her heart stammered. As a starry-eyed teenager she'd fantasized about spending the rest of her life with Ryan. But then reality kicked in, in the form of Janine Lorimer. The woman just couldn't stay sober, could she? Much less resist falling for the charms of yet another good-for-nothing cowboy who'd use her for a while and then leave her in worse shape than he found her.

Shoving thoughts of her mother aside, Grace rose to carry their empty milk glasses to the dishwasher.

Ryan caught her arm. "I can do that. You've had a long day."

"But—"

"Get one thing straight, Grace. You're my wife now, not the maid or the cook or the babysitter. We may have an agreement about the bedroom, but in every other way we're a team."

What could she do but sit back down and let him take the glasses from her hands? He rolled up the sleeves of his dress shirt, the muscles in his tanned forearms flexing as he rinsed the glasses and placed them on the dishwasher rack.

Then, as he squirted dishwasher gel into the dispenser, a thick, gooey blob sprayed out sideways toward Ryan's knees. "Aw, rats. My good pants."

"Oh, no." Grace hurried over and grabbed a paper towel. After dampening it under the faucet, she knelt in front of Ryan and began blotting off the detergent.

"Grace, you don't have to—"

She silenced him with a crooked grin. "We're a team, remember?"

After dabbing up as much as she could, Grace sat back on her heels. "I'd better take these to the dry cleaner's on my way to class tomorrow. Leave them out after you, um…"

Her face suddenly felt hot. She pushed up so quickly

from the floor that she nearly fell backward, and would have if Ryan hadn't caught her hands. The reverse momentum carried her straight into his chest, and they both froze.

Then Ryan's arms surrounded her, while at the same time her arms seemed to fit naturally into the small of his back. Her cheek somehow found its way to the hollow of his shoulder, and beneath his rock-solid chest, his heart thumped a steady rhythm. Slowly, slowly, their breathing synchronized, and the quiet comfort of the moment seemed so right…so perfect.

"Grace." The huskiness in Ryan's voice sounded a warning. "If we stand here like this much longer, I'm not sure I can keep my promise."

For a hair's breadth Grace wasn't sure she wanted him to. *"Trust your heart,"* Linda had told her only a few hours ago.

But that was the problem. How could she trust a heart that had never been taught how to really love a man? How could she trust that she wouldn't someday turn out weak and needy and gullible like her mother—or that Ryan wouldn't grow tired of her and leave her just like all those men her mother had latched on to in search of a little happiness and security?

Foolish, foolish questions, she knew. It didn't take a psychology degree to realize she'd shielded her heart behind a whole passel of what-ifs and improbabilities. But even if none of those things came true, if she allowed herself to love Ryan, to be the wife he desired, there was still one thing that frightened her more than all the rest.

Dear God, what if I fail at being a mother?

"I mean it, Grace." Tenderly Ryan released her and edged away, when everything in him wanted to swoop her into his arms, carry her to the bedroom—*their* bedroom—and show her the depth of his love.

"I'm sorry. I just…" She wouldn't meet his gaze. "It's late, and we both have a lot to do tomorrow. Do you want the bathroom first, or—"

"No, you go ahead."

Grabbing her travel bag off the sofa, she hurried through the living room. The bathroom door clicked shut behind her.

Ryan took a moment to gather his senses before going to the linen closet for a pillow, sheets, and blanket. After shoving the coffee table aside, he made up the sofa bed. Not the world's most comfortable mattress, as his mother had told him every time she'd stayed over, but passable.

The creak of a door hinge announced Grace's exit from the bathroom. "It's all yours," she said before disappearing down the hall.

His brief glimpse of her, ensconced to the neck in a lavender-print flannel robe, her face shining and her hair brushed into smooth waves, brought an ache to his chest. Would she ever be able to love him as he loved her? Would they ever be husband and wife the way God intended?

Later, when Ryan crawled between the sheets and tried to pound his pillow into submission, he could tell he was in for a restless night.

Of course, his trusty alarm clock, in the form of a single-minded four-year-old and her furry, four-legged companion, managed to wake him plenty early the next morning.

"Daddy, it's breakfast time. Get up." Christina jabbed his shoulder. "And Joy needs to go outside to potty."

"Yeah, yeah." Ryan yawned and scraped both hands down his whiskery face. For a second he forgot he'd slept in the living room—and then just as quickly remembered Grace slept down the hall.

That thought prodded him out of bed faster than a red-hot branding iron. He sure didn't need his new bride seeing him in a faded T-shirt and plaid pajama bottoms, not to mention his morning breath, bed head, and desperate need of a shave.

Should he shower first or take the dog out right away? Joy answered with excited yips as she pranced back and forth between him and the door.

"Okay, I'm coming. Christina, you got Joy's leash?" Yawning again and wishing he could crawl back under the covers, Ryan plodded barefoot to the door and tried to pry his eyes open while his daughter clipped the leash on Joy's collar.

She handed him the leash. "Hurry up. I'm hungry."

"Yes, your majesty." Ryan gave her a sleepy salute before braving the early-morning chill.

Dewy grass tickled his feet, and a hummingbird buzzed him on its way to the feeder in the yard next door. While Joy tiptoed across the lawn like the spoiled princess she was, Ryan breathed in the clear, crisp scents of springtime.

A verse from Revelation popped into his head: *He who was seated on the throne said, "I am making everything new!"*

That's what Ryan's life felt like this morning. New. Changed for the better. Filled with a hope he hadn't experienced in a long, long time. The situation with him and Grace was far from perfect, but she'd married him. Right there in front of the pastor and their families and friends, right there in front of God, she'd said, "I do."

If it took him the rest of his life, he'd build a bridge into her heart. He'd tear down every barrier that stood between them until she could finally look into his eyes and say the words he was more convinced than ever she kept locked away deep inside: *I love you.*

Chapter 12

I love you.

The words flitted across Grace's mind as she watched Ryan climb into his pickup and back the farrier trailer down the driveway. He'd left on his calls immediately after a hurried breakfast of cold cereal. Grace had thrust a travel mug of hot coffee in his hand as he flew out the door.

Her cheek still tingled where he'd brushed it with an oh-so-gentle thank-you kiss.

Absently touching the spot, Grace latched the door and turned to see Christina spreading out her array of horse books across the kitchen table. Tongue teasing the corner of her mouth, the little girl flipped through the pages, intent on whatever she searched for.

Still in her robe, Grace ambled over and rested a hand on Christina's shoulder. "Will you be okay here while I shower and dress?"

"The water gets very hot. Never turn the faucet past the little red mark on the wall."

No doubt the warning Ryan had repeated many times to his little girl. Grace smiled. "Thanks, I'll remember that."

A short time later, dressed in jeans and an embroidered knit shirt, Grace returned to the kitchen with her own satchel of books. As she pulled out a chair across from Christina, she glanced at the child's incredibly accurate drawing of a draft horse pulling a cart. "What a great picture, Christina! Mind if we work together for a while? I have a big test to study for."

Christina flicked her pencil rapidly, her tiny mouth twisting into a worried frown. "There are only two possible outcomes, so we'd better pass the test."

Stomach tightening, Grace pushed her textbook aside. "Honey, did you hear your daddy say that?"

"He told the man on the phone."

The man must be Ryan's attorney. No doubt they'd been discussing the social worker's visits.

The girl's breathing quickened. She leaped from the chair. "Joy? Joy Bear! Come out now! Where are you?"

"It's okay. She's here somewhere." Sensing Christina's sudden distress, Grace rose to follow.

Just then, Joy trotted out from Christina's bedroom. The little dog peered up at both of them as if to ask why they'd disturbed her beauty sleep.

"Joy Bear." Christina shook her finger at the dog, her voice growing more shrill with every word. "You must never, never, *never* go anywhere without telling me. It's too dangerous. You could get hurt or lost. What would I ever do without you?"

Grace thrust a hand to her heart, imagining Ryan uttering those same words to Christina the day he thought she'd gotten lost at the farm. When Christina swept the little dog into her arms and hugged her until she squeaked, Grace knelt beside them and gently rescued Joy. "It's all right, sweetie. Joy's safe, and so are you."

But an hour later, when the doorbell rang and a woman introduced herself as a court-appointed social worker, Grace seriously questioned the truth of those words.

"I don't believe we've met." The tall, thin woman, who'd said her name was Nora Purvis, stepped through the front door as if she owned the place. "Are you the babysitter?"

"Not exactly. I'm Mrs. O'Keefe." Merely saying the name aloud gave Grace a strange sense of power.

Nora Purvis's eyes widened, but both her smile and her tone dripped sugary Southern sweetness. "I thought Mr. O'Keefe was unmarried."

"Until yesterday he was." Grace drew up the corners of her mouth with affected cordiality. "Would you care to sit down, Ms. Purvis? May I offer you some coffee or iced tea?"

"No, thank you." Looking flustered, the social worker consulted the thick folder she'd pulled from her briefcase. "Well, I suppose if you're the new Mrs. O'Keefe, you're aware of the custody proceedings Christina's maternal grandparents have initiated."

"Quite aware." Folding her arms, Grace tapped an index finger against the opposite elbow. "And I'd appreciate it if you'd keep your voice down." She nodded toward Christina's bedroom, where the little girl now played.

Ms. Purvis closed her eyes briefly, a look of acquiescence softening her features. "Of course. The last thing I want to do is upset Christina. However, I have a job to do, and meeting you this morning presents an unexpected complication."

"I'm sure it does."

While the social worker took rapid notes, Grace answered every question with as much confidence as she could muster. She told about meeting Ryan as a teenager then going their separate ways for a time but that they'd always remained close friends. She explained how difficult it had been for Ryan to give up hope for a lasting relationship with Christina's mother but that after Shana's death he and Grace had begun to explore their feelings again—none of which was far from the truth.

"Our marriage might seem sudden." Grace twisted the simple gold band Ryan had slipped on her finger yesterday. "But as I said, Ryan and I have known each other for many years."

Ms. Purvis turned a page in her notebook. "So…you had discussed marriage prior to the Burches' filing of the custody suit?"

"Not directly, but…" Grace shifted, looking straight into the social worker's eyes. "Ms. Purvis, you seem like a person who really cares about kids, so I know you want what's best for Christina."

The woman nodded but leaned slightly away, her mouth firm.

"Then believe me when I say I married Ryan because I care deeply about him and about Christina. I want to help Ryan make the best possible home for his little girl, and I'll do whatever it takes to make sure he—to make sure *we* can keep her."

"I respect that, Mrs. O'Keefe, and I understand your position." Ms. Purvis closed her notebook and laced her hands on the cover. "But you must also understand mine. I'm required to report my impartial observations as to the quality and consistency of care this child receives. I can offer recommendations, but ultimately the decision rests upon the judge."

The woman stood. "Now, if you don't mind, I need to spend some time with Christina."

Grace minded. She minded very, very much. But in this instance, passive cooperation seemed the wisest course. She stood hugging herself as Ms. Purvis strode toward Christina's room.

The woman's lilting voice echoed in the hallway. "Hello, Christina. Remember me? We visited last week."

It took every ounce of restraint for Grace to stay rooted where she stood instead of tiptoeing toward the hall to eavesdrop. Suddenly drowning in helplessness and dread, she chewed her lip and wished Ryan were home.

Ryan wrapped up his last appointment of the morning in record time. He sure didn't want to mess up his first day of married life by making his wife late for her afternoon college classes. Pulling into the driveway at home and seeing Grace's silver-blue Yaris there, he felt a surge of anticipation. He pictured himself breezing through the back door to find his gorgeous new bride in the kitchen with a welcoming smile on her face and the aroma of something piping hot and delicious on the table.

The reality didn't quite live up to his fantasy.

"Christina's had lunch, and there's a sandwich for you in the fridge." Grace grabbed her purse, book satchel, and keys. "I should be back by six." She halted halfway through the door. "Oh, and Ms. Purvis was here. I'll tell you about it later."

Stomach lurching at the name he'd come to dread, Ryan spun on his boot heel. "Grace, wait! What did she—"

Too late. Grace waved over her shoulder as she darted around the pickup and climbed into her car. Seconds later she drove away.

Christina toe-walked into the kitchen, Joy prancing along

at her side. She opened the fridge and handed Ryan his sandwich. "Ham and cheese is nutritious and delicious."

Ryan accepted it with a smirk. "Thank you, Rachel Ray."

"Who?"

"Never mind, sweetie." After washing his hands at the sink, Ryan poured himself a glass of iced tea and carried his lunch to the sofa. He had an appointment with Stan Turner this afternoon. Maybe the attorney could shed new light on Ms. Purvis's latest house call and where the custody suit stood.

Except two hours later, with Christina drawing pictures in the law office lobby, Ryan didn't feel at all reassured by Stan's report.

"I wish I could be more encouraging, Ryan. I've talked with the Burches' lawyers at length, and they simply won't back down."

"Then...this is going to court?"

"I'm afraid so." Stan twirled a fancy gold pen between his fingers. "I know you were counting on your marriage to Grace to make a difference, but it may be too little, too late."

"Then tell me, Stan." Fatigue laced Ryan's tone. "Just tell me what I'm gonna have to do to keep my little girl."

"As I've said from the beginning, you're on the defensive here. The Burches will do everything they can to prove you're an unfit parent. You've got to do everything in your power to prove them wrong."

"What do you think I've been doing?" Ryan slid forward and hammered Stan's desk with one clenched fist. "And how could a judge think the Burches should raise Christina when they blew it so bad with their own daughter?"

"That's hearsay. Besides, considering Shana died a hero, one could argue they raised her well." Stan rose and sidled around to Ryan's side of the desk. "I don't mean to imply your case is hopeless. I'm just trying to prepare you for the uphill battle we're facing." He clapped Ryan on the shoulder. "You're a man of faith, right? Keep praying, and keep being the great father I know you are. And keep believing God is in control."

Truth be told, faith was the only thing keeping Ryan halfway sane through all this. With all his being he believed God had the power to keep his family together. Now, with Grace by his side, his family was complete, and he wasn't about to let anything…or anyone…tear them apart.

Please, Father, he prayed as he buckled Christina into her car seat for the drive home, *give me the wisdom I need to fight this battle and win. And when it's over, give me the strength to forgive the Burches for what they've put us through.*

While he was at it, he prayed for the Burches' healing from grief and their guilt over how they'd failed Shana, because he grew more and more convinced that this custody suit had much more to do with the Burch family's past than with Christina's future.

They'd driven only a couple of blocks when Ryan's cell phone buzzed. He snapped it off his belt and checked the caller ID. "Hey, Mr. Tatum. What can I do for you?"

"Darby's thrown a shoe, and we're leaving first thing in the morning for a horse show in West Virginia. Any chance you can come by this afternoon?"

Ryan's chest caved. This was exactly the situation he'd been dreading. Mrs. Airhart was out of town, and Grace wouldn't be home for another two hours. He glanced at Christina through the rearview mirror as he weighed his options. Nope, no way he'd take a chance on word getting back to the Burches that he'd taken his daughter on a farrier call.

"I'm sorry, Mr. Tatum," Ryan said, "but the earliest I could get there would be six thirty. Is that too late?"

"That'll be fine. See you then."

"Darby wears a size four aluminum shoe," Christina stated. She moaned softly. "Darby has a big white star and is very gentle."

Sensing her unspoken disappointment, Ryan bit back the stream of ugly words raging through his brain. All because of the Burches, he had to deny his little girl—and himself— the simple joy of spending their days together while he worked with the horses. He couldn't even imagine the kind of life Christina would have if the Burches were awarded custody. Yeah, they'd give her the best that money could buy. The best in *their* opinion, naturally. Which would prob- ably include a fancy private school where she'd be sheltered and pigeonholed and maybe never reach her full potential.

"Daddy! Red means stop!"

Startled, he snapped back to the present in time to avoid running a traffic signal. "Good catch, sweetie. Sorry about that."

Wandering thoughts were just one more reason he needed this custody suit behind him.

Arriving at home, Ryan backed the truck up the drive- way so he could hitch up his farrier trailer and be ready to leave as soon as Grace returned. And, since she'd been so thoughtful to make him a sandwich before she left for school, the least he could do was have supper on the table when she got home.

Too bad he was a much better farrier than he was a cook.

While he put together a meal of baked chicken breasts, steamed green beans, and prepackaged garlic bread slices, he had Christina do her expert job of setting the table. With the added touch of fresh place mats, a couple of candles, and a jelly-jar vase filled with Mrs. Airhart's pansies, Ryan nodded his approval. Not too shabby a finale for his first full day as a married man.

Then, when six o'clock came and went with no sign of

Grace, Ryan became antsy. He checked his cell to make sure he hadn't missed a call or text. At ten after, he called.

"Sorry, I got stuck in traffic. I should be there in another ten minutes."

In ten minutes, Ryan needed to be out the door and on his way to the Tatums'. "I hate to do this to you, but I've gotta leave as soon as you get here." He explained about Darby. "Supper's ready, though. You and Christina can start without me, and I'll grab something later."

So much for romancing his new bride over dinner, such as it was. He hoped this day wouldn't turn out to be typical of their life together, the proverbial two ships passing in the night. How was he supposed to win Grace's heart if they never spent time together?

What a roller coaster of a day! Waking up a married woman, spending a quiet morning with her stepdaughter, defending her new family to a social worker, and then acing the exam she'd been dreading for the past week.

And now the second-most romantic dinner Grace had ever been invited to, only the man she should be dining with was rushing out the door.

"Shouldn't take long," Ryan said, brushing her cheek with a kiss. He tousled Christina's hair. "Take care of Grace for me, punkin."

"Grace is supposed to take care of *me*."

Grace took Christina's hand. "How about we take care of each other?"

"And Joy, too."

"Oh, we won't forget Joy." Chuckling, Grace offered Ryan a regretful smile. "Thanks for making dinner. I'll keep some warm for you."

Was this the way their lives would always be? Quick kisses hello and good-bye? Probably safer that way, though.

The less time they spent together, the easier it would be to avoid temptation.

But exactly whose temptation concerned her—Ryan's, or her own? How much, really, would she be risking if she let herself love him?

The answer jolted her: *Everything. You'd be risking it all.*

The next several days brought more of the same. On weekdays, Grace stayed home with Christina in the mornings, which allowed her plenty of time to wrap up her semester coursework and study for exams. Ryan scheduled as many appointments as possible for the morning hours or else in the evenings after supper so he could be home with Christina while Grace drove into Charlotte for classes.

Even the weekend kept them busy, what with the barbecue cook-off on Saturday, worship on Sunday, then a Sunday afternoon family gathering at Nathan and Filipa's house before Linda and Tom left the next day for the long drive back to Texas.

The following Wednesday, Grace walked in the door to find the table set with flowers and candles—again—and her heart clenched. She dropped her purse and satchel on a chair. "Ryan…"

He set a large foil takeout container in the center of the table. "Thought we'd celebrate your last final. How'd it go?"

"Pretty good, I think." Last final. Right. This gesture had *nothing* to do with the fact that they'd been married exactly one week tonight. Then her stomach rumbled at the delicious aroma filling the air. "What is that?"

"Chicken Alfredo, à la Kingsley Station. Christina and I picked it up this afternoon on the way home from Stan's office." Ryan struck a match and lit the candles then pulled out Grace's chair. "May I seat you, Mrs. O'Keefe?"

Noticing Ryan appeared freshly showered and without

even a hint of five o'clock shadow, Grace suddenly felt grungy in her polo shirt and faded jeans. "I should wash up first."

Maybe a few minutes in the bathroom would calm the jitters Ryan always managed to evoke.

After running a brush through her hair and redoing her ponytail, she felt somewhat more presentable. As Ryan helped her into her chair, she asked softly, "How was your meeting with Stan?"

Later, he mouthed, tipping his head toward Christina. His forced smile was far from reassuring.

Grace glanced up with concern, but when his fingers traced her nape as he moved to take his own seat, she couldn't suppress a shiver. Did he have any idea his thoughtfulness and gentle touches only made it harder to remember this marriage was a... She hesitated to call it a business arrangement. More of a cooperative effort—two friends helping each other.

Whatever they called this relationship, at least between themselves, Grace decided Ryan knew exactly what his nearness did to her, and he obviously intended to take full advantage.

At least as far as Grace would allow.

Halfway through dinner, Grace's cell phone chirped from the depths of her purse. Recognizing the personalized ringtone, Grace squeezed her eyes shut. A sick sense of dread swamped her. "Please. Not tonight."

Ryan laid aside his fork and reached out to her. "Grace?"

"That's my mother's ring. If she's calling, it can only be trouble."

"Let me get it." Ryan started to rise.

"No. She's my problem, not yours." Grace snatched her purse off the chair and tugged out the phone.

Ryan stopped her before she answered. "That's where

you're wrong. Remember? For better or for worse, we're in this together."

Huffing a resigned breath, she nodded and took the call. "What is it, Mother?"

"Oh, honey, Mama nee's her girl. Mama nee's her bad."

The slurred voice meant only one thing: Janine Lorimer had fallen off the wagon. Again.

Not willing to subject either Ryan or Christina to this conversation, Grace pushed up from the table and took the phone out to the back porch. "What are you on this time? Booze? Pills? Crack?"

"I'm tryin', honey, but—" Erratic sobs sounded in Grace's ear. "He hit me! I can't stay with him no more!"

Collapsing against the side of the house, Grace massaged her temple. "Are you still in Vegas? Don't you have a friend or somebody you can go to?"

"I got no one, don't you un'erstand? You're all I got."

The pleading, childlike whimpers made Grace cringe. She could easily understand why Kip had fled Texas to start anew in North Carolina, hoping Janine would never find him again. "I can't help you, Mother. How many times do we have to go through this?"

"Le' me come stay with you awhile, Grace. All's I need is a little money for a plane ticket, an' I'll—"

"No. I'm…I'm married now. I have a family to think about."

"M–married? My girl's *married*?" More sobs. "First Kip, now you. You got no respect for your own mother, not invitin' me to the wedding, not even the courtesy to tell me till it's over and done!" Janine drew a rattling breath. "Well, mark my words, Miss High-and-Mighty. God'll give you your comeuppance for treatin' your mama this way! You're gonna learn quick that men don't want nothin' 'cept a woman they can use as they please and then toss aside. Which is exactly what you deserve, you ungrateful—"

Hands shaking, tears drenching her face, Grace thrust the phone away and stabbed the disconnect button. She should never have told her mother about the wedding, should never have answered the call in the first place. *Why, Mother? Why do you always have to suck every last hope of happiness from my life?*

She hardly heard the back door click shut before finding herself wrapped in Ryan's strong arms. His soothing voice tunneled through her rage until it found her heart. "It's okay, angel-babe. I've got you now. It's okay."

Chapter 13

Two days later, Ryan still couldn't get over how one stinkin' phone call could come near to destroying such a confident, giving, beautiful woman. He'd like to get hold of Janine Lorimer and shake some sense into her alcohol-befuddled brain.

And while he was at it, maybe he'd shake Harold and Irene Burch off their catbird seat. What was it with these people? The Burches thought money could buy love, while Janine Lorimer's currency was guilt. They'd all failed miserably, and yet they were too blind or else too stubborn to see where they'd gone wrong.

"Grace hasn't been the same since your mom called," Ryan told Kip as he worked the rasp across Gem's left rear hoof. "I don't know how to help her."

With a disgusted snort, Kip adjusted his Stetson. "Janine's hopeless. I hardly ever answer her calls anymore. I'm sorry she's still bothering Grace."

Ryan paused and angled his friend a curious glance. "Never thought I'd hear you say *anybody*'s hopeless. Aren't you always reminding me God can do anything?"

"I know He can." Kip set his jaw. "I'm just startin' to doubt He will."

Ryan set Gem's hoof on the barn floor. Straightening, he eased the kinks out of his back. With all the pain and disappointment surrounding him, with all the problems in his own life, it would be easy for Ryan to lose hope, to believe God didn't care.

"I can't let myself think that way, not for a minute," Ryan said as he carted his tool kit around to Gem's other side. "If I did, I'd go crazy."

Kip sighed. "Don't listen to me. I'm just blowin' off steam. I know God's in control. But every time I see another pregnancy test wrapper in the bathroom trash, it feels like my insides are gonna split open. I don't know how much more of this we can take."

Ryan clamped his teeth together and focused harder on his work. How many times had he asked himself—asked God—why Kip and Sheridan had been trying for years to have a baby, and all it took for him and Shana was one reckless night?

Excusing himself to tend to other chores, Kip called Manuelo into the barn to help Ryan with the other three horses due for a hoof trim. Ryan finished quickly and found he had time to run home for lunch before his next appointment. It would be nice to surprise Grace and Christina, and maybe he could cheer up Grace a bit. Bad enough she'd been down ever since her mother called, but staying home with Christina all day until summer classes started at UNC, she seemed at loose ends.

The house was quiet and dark as a cave when Ryan let

himself in the back door. Squinting into the shadowy living room, he called softly, "Grace? You here?"

A motion on the sofa caught his eye. Grace sat up slowly, dropping something into her lap. "What are you doing home?" she asked hoarsely.

He hurried over and edged onto the sofa beside her, pressing the back of his hand to her forehead. "What's wrong, honey? Are you sick?"

"No, no, just a headache. It's been a rough morning." She brushed his hand aside. Rising, she tossed a damp washcloth onto the coffee table and then went to open the living room blinds.

Ryan's first thought was that the social worker had come by again. Stomach churning, he glanced around, suddenly aware of Christina's absence. "What happened?"

"Mrs. Airhart's back in town." Grace's mouth quirked as she plopped into the easy chair across from Ryan. "Christina was very unhappy to see Joy leave, and she threw an ugly tantrum."

"Aw, man." Ryan scrubbed his hands over his eyes. "You should have called me."

"There was no reason for you to cancel your appointments and come home. It's fine. We survived."

By the looks of his bedraggled wife, *surviving* was about all she'd managed. "Where's Christina now?"

"Asleep. I finally got her calmed down by reminding her Joy was right next door and they could visit anytime. Then I read to her awhile, fed her some lunch, and she was ready for a nap."

Exactly how Ryan would have handled it. He breathed out a relieved sigh and then went to sit on the arm of Grace's chair. Pulling her gently against his chest, he kissed the top of her head. She relaxed against him for a moment, and he relished their closeness, wishing it would last. "Thank you. It means everything to know you're here taking care of our little girl."

Our little girl. The word choice wasn't lost on Grace. Neither was the fact that Ryan had started using endearments like *honey* and *sweetie* when he spoke to her. A far cry from *squirt*.

And when had she ceased even thinking of calling him *scuzzy*?

Abruptly she pushed up from the chair. "Did you come home for lunch? Let me fix you something."

"You're the one with the headache. Sit back down." Ryan took her damp cloth to the sink to freshen it. Returning, he nudged her onto the sofa, arranged her pillows, and helped her lie back. Then, perched on the narrow space beside her, he patted her face with the cool washcloth.

"Ryan…"

"Don't argue with your husband, Mrs. O'Keefe." His cajoling grin silenced her. He simply would not let her forget she was his wife now, and a part of her was glad.

So this was what it meant to have a man love you, sacrifice for you, care for you like no one else on earth. This was how Kip loved Sheridan, how Nathan loved Filipa. It was how Grace had always dreamed of being loved…and doubted she ever would be.

A tear slid down her cheek. Ryan blotted the moisture away with the washcloth. "What's that for?" he asked.

"You," she murmured. "You're too good to me, Ryan."

He dropped to his knees beside the sofa and eased one arm beneath her shoulders so that their faces hovered only inches apart. "Nothing's too good for the woman who owns my heart."

Her throat closed. She blinked several times, sending more wetness down her cheek. "I wish… I wish…"

Ryan kissed each tear away, his lips searing them like tender flames. "Just say it, Grace. Say you love me."

Heat suffused her face. Her heart clutched in agony, but she couldn't say the words. Shoving herself upright, she fought for breath. "I want to, but—"

"I know you're scared. And I know it's because of your mom." Ryan edged up beside her but thankfully didn't torture her by trying to hold her again. "Kip got past her mistakes and found happiness. You can, too."

"It's different. She didn't raise him. I've spent most of my life watching her ruin her own, and even when she tries to get it right, she always fails."

"And you think that means you'll fail, too?"

"If I ever let you down, ever did anything to hurt Christina, I could never forgive myself." She shot him a desperate glance then tore her eyes away. "And I can't take that chance."

"It's a chance I'm willing to take—a chance I've already taken, and so have you, if you'd just admit it." Ryan caught her hands, his thumb tracing the thin gold band on her left ring finger. "You're my wife now, Grace. Let me be your husband…in every sense of the word."

"Ryan, you promised." The words scraped her throat raw. She tugged her hands away and stood. Even when she scurried to the kitchen and rifled through the refrigerator for sandwich makings, he felt too close, as if invisible bonds connected them. "Smoked ham or pastrami? Do you want lettuce or—"

"Grace." He moved beside her again, forcing her to set the lunch items on the counter and close the refrigerator door. "I can make my own sandwich, okay? Just go lie down." Frustration and fatigue laced his tone. He huffed as he pulled two slices of bread from the wrapper. He took a knife from the drawer and then slammed the drawer shut.

The sound made Grace wince. She stood by the table, arms folded across her ribs. "This isn't going to work, is it?"

Ryan laid the knife aside with a groan. He pressed his knuckles into the countertop and dropped his chin to his chest. Then quietly, stiffly, he repackaged the bread slices and put everything away. Striding past Grace without so much as a parting glance, he collected his keys from the table and left.

An eternity passed while Grace struggled to suppress the tremors coursing through her. She felt cold all over. Cold and empty and alone.

Only when a tiny hand tugged at her shirttail did she find the strength to move again. She looked down into Christina's curious green eyes and pasted on a forced smile. "Hi, honey. Did you have a good nap?"

"I slept one hour and twelve minutes. Read me more from the palomino book now." Christina thrust a big storybook into Grace's hands. Then, almost like an afterthought, she added, "Please and thank you."

Obviously a lesson in politeness Ryan had been teaching his little girl. Grace pushed aside the remnants of her despair and guided Christina over to the sofa. "Okay, where were we?"

"Page twenty-seven." Christina crawled onto the cushions and sat hip to hip with Grace then pointed to the exact spot where Grace had stopped reading earlier. "This is the part when the mare has her baby. It's a colt. That's a boy horse."

"Right." Grace continued the story, although she suspected Christina already had the entire book memorized.

When the story ended, Christina drew her knees up and propped the closed book on her legs. She patted the cover, which depicted a beautiful golden palomino frolicking with a colt. "Mother horses have to take care of their foals. The sire doesn't, though."

"That's true." Grace had the feeling there was more to Christina's comment than horse facts.

"My daddy takes care of me and you take care of me." Christina tipped her head to gaze up at Grace. "My other mommy is in heaven. I'm going to call you Mommy now."

Before Grace could hitch a breath, Christina bounded off the sofa to fetch her drawing tablet.

A conspiracy, that's what it was. First Ryan and now his daughter. Whatever misguided sense of altruism had landed Grace in this marriage, she'd somehow managed to block out the whole "till death parts us" aspect. Seriously, had she really thought she could waltz in, save Christina from her grandparents' clutches, then simply walk away from Ryan and continue her life as if none of this had ever happened?

Hearts were at stake here. Ryan's, Christina's…and now her own. If Grace wasn't careful, she'd end up hurting them all.

"I'm not made of stone."

Had he just said that out loud? Ryan shifted his gaze left and right, relieved the other customers in the greeting card aisle hadn't appeared to notice.

"Daddy, we needed milk and frozen waffles." Christina flapped her hands. "We need to go to the milk-and-frozen-waffles row."

"Yeah, sugarplum, I know. Hang on a sec." It was Saturday morning, and while Grace taught her classes at Cross Roads Farm, Ryan had run to the supermarket to pick up a few things. He'd been blindsided by a huge display at the entrance reminding him tomorrow was Mother's Day.

Every year since Christina was born, Ryan had hand-picked a special card for Shana. The early ones had contained tender, romantic sentiments, his not-so-subtle way of letting her know he still hoped they could be together. As he grew to accept that Shana would never change her mind about marriage, he gave up on sentimentality and stuck to humorous reminders that she'd always be the mother of their little girl.

He'd thought about going the humor route with Grace—anything to ease the tension between them and reassure her he respected her feelings and would never go back on his word. Yesterday had been a killer, and he still wanted to kick himself for losing his cool and walking out. By evening they'd both chilled out some, or at least wanted each other to believe they had. But Ryan hadn't been able to get Grace's words out of his mind: *"This isn't going to work, is it?"*

"Look, Daddy. A picture of Joy." Christina pointed to a greeting card featuring one of those fish-eye lens photos of a dog's face. A pink tongue protruded between Pomeranian doggy lips drawn back in a semblance of a grin. *I woof you this much*, the card read. Christina screwed up the corner of her mouth. "That isn't how you spell *love*."

Close enough—or as close as Ryan dared go. And maybe this particular card would also convey how sorry he was about yesterday and how much he appreciated what Grace had gone through with Christina. He plucked the card and envelope from the rack. "Okay, kiddo, let's find the milk and waffles."

Grace arrived home as Ryan carried a batch of laundry to the washer. "How were your classes?" he asked.

"Fine." She plopped onto a kitchen chair to unlace her paddock boots.

Christina sat at the table with her sketchbook. "I woof you. I woof you. I woof you," she repeated in a monotone. "This is Joy's tail, and this is Joy's paw, and this is Joy's ear."

"We should go over and visit Joy later." Grace set her boots by the back door. "But I need a shower first."

Ryan nodded toward the laundry basket he held. "Toss me your jeans and I'll throw them in with this load."

Momentary discomfort flickered behind Grace's eyes. "Thanks." She started toward the bathroom. "I won't be long. I know you need to head out on appointments."

Apparently they were still walking the thin line of polite reserve. Ryan looked forward to tomorrow, his first opportunity to enjoy an entire uninterrupted day with his wife and daughter—*enjoy* being the operative word. *Please, Lord, let it be so.*

Grace awoke Sunday morning to a light tapping on the bedroom door. She tugged the covers around her. "Yes?"

Christina pushed the door open and toe-walked over to the bed. "Daddy said to wake you up. We made you breakfast."

"Breakfast?" Shoving tangles off her face, Grace shifted upward in the bed.

"Orange juice, coffee, waffles, butter, syrup. I pushed the button on the toaster." Christina climbed onto the end of the bed and dangled her legs off the side.

"Knock, knock." Ryan's voice echoed from the hallway. "Ready or not, here I come."

Grace barely had time to adjust her pillow and straighten her sleep shirt before Ryan marched in carrying a tray. After giving her a moment to smooth the covers, he set the tray across her lap. A single red rose in a bud vase adorned one corner. "Breakfast is served, Mrs. O'Keefe. Happy Mother's Day."

She breathed in the tempting aromas of maple syrup, melted butter, and freshly brewed coffee. She'd remembered today was Mother's Day, but she'd never expected this kind of treatment! Unexpectedly her eyes welled up.

Ryan handed her a tissue from the nightstand. "Hey, you haven't even tasted it yet."

She couldn't help but laugh. "I'm sure it's wonderful. But you really shouldn't—"

"Don't want to hear it." Waggling a chiding finger, Ryan backed away. "You just eat up and enjoy while I shower and shave, and then the bathroom's yours." At the doorway he swung around with a teasing grin. "Oh, and by the way, my turn's coming. Father's Day is just around the corner."

"If you think I'm serving *you* breakfast in bed—"

"Already working on my menu requests." The bedroom door thudded closed.

Shaking her head, Grace looked at Christina. "Is he serious?"

Christina only shrugged. Hopping off the bed, she tiptoed to the dresser and quietly began aligning Grace's things.

With a sigh, Grace decided that since Ryan and Christina had gone to so much trouble, the least she could do was eat the waffles before they grew cold. As for Father's Day, she'd cross that bridge when she came to it.

She soon learned that breakfast in bed wasn't the only surprise Ryan had in store. After church he took her and Christina for lunch at a colorful little Mexican restaurant on the edge of Charlotte then drove across town to the Carolina Raptor Center. They spent the afternoon walking the trails and viewing the amazing variety of wild birds on exhibit.

Long before they reached home, Christina had fallen asleep in her car seat, and Ryan had to carry her inside. With Grace's help, he tucked her into bed to finish her nap then invited Grace to join him on the sofa for a cold drink.

"So how was your first official Mother's Day?" Ryan asked as he handed her a frosty glass of cola.

"Never felt so pampered in my life." Grace sipped slowly, enjoying the way the bubbles tickled her nose. With a rippling sigh, she said, "Thank you, Ryan. Really. It was wonderful."

"I'm glad." He tucked her free hand in his, but when she tensed, he gave her fingers a gentle squeeze. "Just holdin' hands here. Nothin' else goin' on."

She made herself relax. Ryan deserved so much better than the way things had been between them. "Can we talk about…us?"

He shifted slightly. "Nothin' I'd like better."

After setting her glass on the coffee table, Grace scooted into the corner of the sofa and faced Ryan. Still, she resisted meeting his gaze. "I know I've been hard to live with the past few days. All this—" She flung her hands in a gesture meant to encompass Ryan, Christina, the whole idea of being a wife and mother. "It's been overwhelming, to say the least. I don't think I fully comprehended what I was signing on for."

Ryan's jaw muscles bunched. He set his glass down with a *thunk*. "If you want out—"

"That isn't what I'm saying."

He cast a nervous glance toward her. "I just thought—"

"Will you let me finish, please?"

"Sorry." Ryan splayed his hands across his thighs, index fingers tapping nervously.

Tucking one leg under her, Grace examined a spot on her jeans while she tried to order her thoughts. All day long she'd been silently evaluating exactly where this relationship was headed, because she knew continuing as they'd begun would be impossible. And not only because it wasn't fair to Ryan or Christina but because Grace was beginning to realize how horribly unfair she was being to herself.

"What I'm trying to say," she murmured then bit her lip. Getting the words out was so much harder than she'd expected. Finally she blurted out, "The thing is, Ryan, I always knew deep inside that if ever I did get married, you'd be the one. There's no one else on earth I could ever care for like I care for you."

At Ryan's sharp gasp, she peeked up to see the hopeful smile lighting his eyes. Quickly she glanced away—still so much more she needed to say. "But then you met Shana, and I can't even describe how jealous and hurt I felt. When I heard she was having your baby, I knew for certain I'd never have another chance with you. And even now that Shana's gone…I still wonder, if she'd come home alive, if—if—"

"Stop right now and come here." Ryan drew her into his arms and pressed her head against his shoulder. "Don't you get it, Grace? It's always been you. Always. But we were both mixed-up kids trying to find our way in the world, and we didn't always make good choices."

The gentle throb of Ryan's heartbeat pulsed against Grace's cheek. "You weren't in love with Shana?"

"I loved her, yeah. She helped me through a rough time in my life when I was still sorting things out. But as much as I cared for Shana, I couldn't seem to fill up the emptiness in her. Though I denied it for a long time, I think getting married would have been a huge mistake."

Grace sat up, resting one hand against Ryan's chest as she searched his eyes. "I don't want us to be a mistake. I want to make this work."

Chapter 14

After Christina's riding class at Cross Roads Farm Tuesday evening, Ryan let Sheridan take Christina inside for milk and cookies while he followed Grace to the barn. Since Sunday, he'd found it harder than ever to keep his distance from the woman he loved. They still needed to work through a few issues before Grace finally accepted Ryan as her husband, but things were definitely moving in the right direction.

Grace peered at Ryan over Belle's stall door, a teasing grin turning up one side of her mouth. "Are you following me?"

"Could be." Ryan grinned back.

"Then make yourself useful." Grace hefted Belle's saddle across the gate. "And hand me the grooming tote while you're at it."

"Bossy thing, aren't ya?" After passing her the tote, Ryan lugged the saddle to the tack room.

Nathan met him coming through the door. "Hey, stranger." He winked. "Planning that honeymoon yet?"

"We'll get around to it." Edging around the big man, Ryan set the saddle on an empty rack. The hope that Grace might actually agree to a real honeymoon before much longer bloomed brighter every day.

Growing serious, Nathan said, "I don't blame you for waiting till things settle down some. What's the latest with the custody suit?"

The reminder brought an unwelcome twinge to Ryan's belly. "The social worker's still doing interviews. She asked for a full list of my clients and personal references."

Kip ambled through the door with two bridles and a saddle pad. "You talking about that Ms. Purvis lady? She was here yesterday."

"Great." Ryan ground his teeth together. "Can I ask what she said? What *you* said?"

"She asked how long I've known you, my opinion of your character, that kind of stuff. I told her there's not a more upstanding, honest, selfless person on the face of the earth."

"Hey, now!" Nathan slapped Kip playfully on the arm. "What about your upstanding, honest, and utterly selfless brother-in-law? What am I, chopped liver?"

Kip massaged his arm, grimacing as if it hurt way more than Nathan intended. "See, that's exactly why they say you can pick your friends, but you can't pick your family."

Right then, Ryan was plenty glad he'd picked both Kip and Nathan as friends. Without them in his corner, this custody battle would be a whole lot tougher.

After thanking Kip for vouching for him, Ryan left the tack room to find Grace. "Ready to head home, sweetie?"

"Sounds good." Her welcoming smile melted his heart. "Why don't you get Christina, and I'll gather a few more of my things from the cottage."

He liked the sound of that. The more of her possessions she moved over to his place, the more confident he felt in her commitment to him and their marriage.

At home later, and with Christina bathed and tucked into bed, Ryan helped Grace hang up the clothing she'd brought over. "These are real nice." He held up a pair of sea-blue cropped pants. "How come I've never seen you wear them?"

"I bought them last year and forgot." Snatching the pants from Ryan's hand, Grace shoved some of his clothes aside and slid the hanger onto the rod. "You've got enough shirts in here for three guys," she teased. "I think we're going to need a bigger closet."

Ryan moved in close, wrapping his arms around Grace's waist and pulling her against him. He smiled into her eyes, thinking of the passel of children he dreamed of having with her. "Maybe what we need is a bigger house."

Her gaze shifted uneasily, but at least she didn't pull away. "I'm sorry about the sofa bed. It's just…before we take the next step, I need to be sure."

"I'm sure enough for both of us." He looked deeply into her eyes. "I'll wait for you, Grace. But don't *ever* doubt how I feel, because I love you so much it hurts." His gaze drifted to her lips, parted so sweetly, questioningly, and he could hardly breathe. Lowering his mouth upon hers, he kissed her with tenderness—a purposeful yet patient kiss meant to invite and encourage.

When her arms snaked around his back and he sensed her giving herself over to the kiss, his heart swelled until he thought it would explode from his chest. Then, with every ounce of restraint he possessed, he loosened his hold and allowed their lips to drift apart. He gazed into half-lidded eyes grown soft and dusky and saw that he'd finally touched her soul.

* * *

Grace never knew the end of a kiss could hurt so much. Everything in her wanted to draw Ryan closer, closer, to savor the masculine sweetness of his lips upon hers. It would be so easy...so very easy...

"Good night, Grace." One hand extended, Ryan backed slowly toward the door.

She uttered a tiny moan, shocked by her body's response to his kiss, stunned that he would leave her now and simply walk away. "Ryan...?"

"Sweet dreams. See you in the mornin', hon." The door clicked shut.

Sweet dreams? Kind of hard to dream when she barely captured a moment of sleep all night! The next morning, standing bleary-eyed before the bathroom mirror, she wasn't sure whether she should strangle Ryan or thank him. He must have sensed her weakening resistance, must have realized how close she'd been to giving herself as his wife in every way...and yet he hadn't pressed his advantage.

Oh, her husband was so much wiser than she'd ever be! Her body may have been willing, but Ryan wanted her heart and mind as well, and he wouldn't settle for anything less.

One day soon, she hoped to give him her all.

After washing her face and gathering her hair into a ponytail, Grace dressed in denim shorts and a summery pink top. She found Ryan in the kitchen pouring a bowl of frosted wheat squares for Christina. He looked freshly shaven, his hair wet and spiky. The sofa bed had been folded up, sheets and pillows stacked at one end.

Amazed Ryan could look so rested after the night she'd had, Grace eyed him with envy as she poured herself a mug of coffee. "How long have you been up?"

"Not long. But I gotta get an early start today. I'm meeting Stan Turner at three." Ryan pulled out a chair and sat down to put on his boots.

Grace carried her coffee to the table and sat across from him. "I hope he has better news this time."

Stirring her breakfast cereal, Christina said loudly, "Horses eat grass, hay, alfalfa, and grains. Sometimes carrots and peppermints for treats."

Ryan cast his daughter a concerned frown then glanced meaningfully at Grace. "Walk me out to the pickup?"

Grace nodded. "Be right back, Christina. Finish your breakfast."

Hurrying barefoot across the damp lawn, Grace followed Ryan's long strides to the driveway. He opened the pickup door and laid his phone, keys, and soft-sided briefcase on the seat then turned and drew Grace into his arms. But his tense sigh told her romance wasn't foremost in his thoughts just now.

She wrapped her arms around him and rubbed his back. "You're worried, aren't you?"

"Can't help it. And I'm scared Christina senses way more than she understands."

"How much longer? When will this be over?"

"Soon, I hope." Ryan kissed her temple before releasing her and climbing into the driver's seat. When he looked her way again, a warm yet mischievous smile had crept into his eyes. "I love you, Mrs. O'Keefe."

Her pulse quickened with the memory of last night's kiss. One hand to her lips, she waved good-bye as Ryan backed down the driveway, and her heart answered, *I love you, too.*

Reluctantly she turned to go inside, already dreading how empty the house would seem without Ryan there.

After making breakfast for herself and then settling Christina in front of the TV to watch one of her favorite horse DVDs, Grace opened her laptop and logged onto the

UNC Charlotte website. Classes started again next Monday, and she wanted to make sure her schedule was in order.

Christina rose from the sofa and leaned against the arm of Grace's chair. She studied the computer screen. "With Skype you can call people anywhere in the world. Even Afghanistan. But not heaven." She frowned, one hand flapping at her side. "Grandpa's computer doesn't have Skype."

Grace could only imagine what frightening thoughts were going through Christina's mind. She closed her laptop and set it on the coffee table. "Do you want to sit with me awhile? We could watch your movie together."

Without answering, Christina climbed into the chair with Grace. Scooting in as close as she could get, she pulled Grace's arm around her so tightly that Grace could feel the little girl's quick breaths and anxious heartbeat. Little by little, as they watched the story of a young boy and his horse, Christina began to relax. Parts of the movie she quoted from memory along with the actors, occasionally correcting some bit of factual information the moviemakers had gotten wrong. Grace could only nod in silent awe.

When the movie ended, Christina asked for another, but before Grace could switch out the DVDs, the doorbell rang. She padded over and peeked through the peephole.

Oh, great. The social worker again.

Steeling herself, Grace opened the door and tried to keep the annoyance out of her voice. "Hello, Ms. Purvis."

"Good morning, Mrs. O'Keefe. Sorry to keep dropping by unannounced, but that's part of my job." The woman's smile looked sincere, as if she really did understand how unnerving her visits could be. She peered around Grace. "Is Mr. O'Keefe at home?"

"No, he's out making farrier calls."

"And Christina?"

Grace opened the door wider and motioned Ms. Purvis

inside. "We've just been watching a movie. You're welcome to join us."

Remaining on the porch, the woman glanced toward the driveway. "Actually, I'm not alone." She handed Grace an official-looking document. "I'm here with the Burches for a court-ordered supervised visit."

Grace stared at the printed page, but the words blurred into gibberish. Nausea rose in her throat. She swallowed painfully. "I need to call Ryan."

"I understand. I'll wait out here with the Burches." Ms. Purvis's expression came as close to being apologetic as her professionalism would allow. "However, I'm afraid the court requires you to comply."

Nodding stupidly, Grace shut the door. Her legs felt numb as she strode over to where she'd left her purse on a kitchen chair. Finding her cell phone, she discovered an hour-old voice mail and realized she hadn't turned the phone off vibrate after last night's classes at Cross Roads Farm. Hurriedly she pressed the button to play back the message.

"This is Stan Turner," the recorded voice said. "I've tried to reach Ryan, but he must not have his cell handy." He went on to explain he'd just received word that morning about the Burches' visit. "It's just a formality, and the social worker is required to be there the whole time, so there's nothing to be overly concerned about. It may even help our case."

Only slightly reassured, Grace called Ryan's number, but after six rings, the call went to his voice mail. Assuming he'd hear Stan's message first, she stated briefly that Ms. Purvis and the Burches had arrived and that she'd call him again as soon as they left. Hopefully he'd check messages before heading to his next appointment.

Shoving the phone into her purse, Grace drew a shaky breath then strode to the living room and knelt beside the chair where Christina sat staring at a blank TV screen.

"Honey, we have company. Your grandparents have come to visit."

Christina stiffened. Her tiny fingers waggled nervously along her thighs. "I want to watch my movie."

"Maybe they'll watch it with you." Rising, Grace rested her hand on Christina's head for a moment. This would be okay. It had to be.

But when she opened the door to admit Ms. Purvis and the Burches, she knew it wouldn't be. Tucked into Irene Burch's arms was a squirming ball of red-gold fur—a Pomeranian puppy.

"That about wraps it up, Mr. Nelson." Ryan gathered his tools while a stable hand led the frisky chestnut mare to her stall. "Give me five minutes and I'll have your bill ready."

Shoulders and back aching after a long morning of routine hoof trims for the wealthy breeder of fine Arabians, Ryan set his tool kit inside the trailer, shut down the forge, and latched the doors. He went to the pickup cab for his briefcase and pulled out his invoice book.

Then, as he prepared to figure up Mr. Nelson's bill, a chime sounded from his phone. He picked it up from the console and checked the readout: six voice mails since he'd arrived at the Nelson place early that morning. His stomach dipped. Probably just clients calling…but what if Grace had needed his help with Christina? He could kick himself for not remembering to check his phone more often.

Before listening to the messages, he viewed the call log. The first two missed calls he recognized as clients. When he saw that the next three were from Stan Turner, followed almost immediately by a call from Grace, his stomach took the express elevator all the way down to his toes. Skipping over the client calls, he went straight to Stan's messages— and tried really hard not to panic.

He made himself listen all the way through, including Grace's voice mail, and then forced himself to take several calming breaths before he returned Grace's call.

"Are they there?" he blurted as soon as she answered. "Right this minute?"

"Ryan, I thought you'd never call." Grace's voice echoed strangely. "They've been here over an hour. And you won't believe this. They brought Christina a puppy."

"A puppy." Ryan slammed his palm against his forehead. "A *puppy*?"

"She looks exactly like a little Joy. Christina went crazy over her." Air whistled through the phone line. "Ryan, can you come home?"

He checked his watch. "I'm all the way over in Rock Hill. It'd take me nearly an hour to get there. How long do you think they'll stay?"

"Awhile yet. Mr. Burch just called for pizza delivery."

Anger boiled in Ryan's gut. A puppy, a pizza—the Burches sure knew how to buy Christina's affection. Next they'd promise her her very own pony.

Hearing boots on gravel, Ryan glanced over his shoulder to see Mr. Nelson waiting patiently, checkbook in hand. Offering an apologetic smile, Ryan turned away and lowered his voice. "Hang in there, sweetie. I'll get home as soon as I can."

Disconnecting, Ryan laid his phone aside and returned to the bill he'd been about to tally. "Let's see, we did Cinnamon, Zsa Zsa, Ricki, and—" His mind blanked.

"Jasmine." Mr. Nelson clicked his ballpoint. "And don't forget Rusty. You did a full set of new shoes for him."

Insides jumping, Ryan fought to keep his hand from shaking as he wrote out the bill. Not daring to total the figures in his head, he reached for his phone and pressed the calculator button.

He'd entered only a couple of numbers when the phone rang. Seeing Turner, Stanley on the caller ID, Ryan tossed aside his pen and took the call. "Stan, what's going on? Christina's still mine, isn't she? Can the Burches just show up like this without my permission? Don't I have the right to say when and if—"

"Easy, Ryan, slow down. I know this is upsetting, but it's all part of the process. And I promise you, the more cooperative you are now, the better position you'll have in the long run."

Ryan noticed Mr. Nelson had backed off a discreet distance. "Yeah, so long as I don't 'cooperate' my little girl straight out of my life."

"It'll be okay, trust me." Stan cleared his throat. "Look, do me—and yourself—a favor, and don't go rushing home. Nora Purvis knows her job, and Grace is there, too. If you barge in doing the 'overprotective daddy' routine, you risk alienating the Burches even more than you already have."

"I've alienated *them*? What about—"

"Ryan, chill out." Stan's tone was firmly insistent. "I want you to continue with your work and plan on keeping your three o'clock appointment with me as scheduled. By then the Burches should be on their way back to Shelby, and you and I can talk strategy for our court date."

Chest aching, Ryan squeezed his eyes shut. "Okay, okay. Just promise me I won't lose my little girl."

Chapter 15

Grace tried to remain inconspicuous while hovering close enough to keep an eye on things in the living room—no easy task when she'd already washed up the breakfast dishes, started the last batch of laundry, skimmed the morning paper, and browsed through the stack of advertising fliers from yesterday's mail. With a pizza delivery expected any minute, she didn't even need to make lunch.

Drinks. She could pour drinks. And it would give her an excuse to casually interrupt.

She sidled into the living room, where Christina sat giggling on the sofa between her grandparents while the puppy scampered from lap to lap. A sinking feeling hollowed the pit of her stomach. Grace could see where this was headed. The more excited Christina became, the worse her eventual meltdown would be.

"I thought I'd start getting things ready for lunch." Grace laced her fingers behind her back. "Would anyone like sweet tea? We also have colas, root beer, lemonade mix…"

"Tea is fine." Mrs. Burch tore her gaze away from Christina and the puppy long enough to offer Grace a quick, if slightly imperious, "Thank you."

Grace nodded. "Ms. Purvis?"

"Just a glass of water, please." The woman's detached expression gave away nothing about her assessment of this visit.

As Grace dispensed ice into drink glasses, her cell phone buzzed in her pocket, and the sudden vibration made her jump. Seeing Ryan's name on the caller ID, she ducked around the corner into the laundry room before answering. "Hey. Are you on your way home?"

Silence. "Uh, no. I just talked to Stan. He says I should stay away."

"But, Ry, this is so awkward for me." Grace sank against the washing machine, one hand covering her eyes.

"I know, hon. But I'm counting on you. I kn— you—"

"Ryan, you're breaking up." Static filled her ear. "Ry?"

"In a —d zone. —Try lat—" The phone beeped with the *call lost* tone.

Frustration eating her alive, Grace tapped the phone against her forehead. How was she to survive the rest of the afternoon without Ryan?

Then the phone buzzed again. Relief flooded Grace when she saw Sheridan's name on the display. At least she could count on her sister-in-law for a sympathetic ear. "Sher, I'm so glad you called. I'm about to—"

"I need your help, Grace."

Grace's head shot up at the urgency in Sheridan's voice. "What's wrong? Are you okay?"

"That's the thing. I don't know." Sheridan released a shaky sigh. "I'm pregnant again."

"Sher, that's wonderful!"

"I haven't told anyone, not even Kip, and a little while ago I started cramping and spotting."

Grace clutched her stomach. "Oh, no."

"It isn't bad yet, but I'm scared. My OB/GYN can see me this afternoon, but I'm too nervous to drive myself. Any chance you could take me?"

Shifting her attention to the laughter coming from the living room, Grace weighed her response. "Isn't Kip at home? He'd want to be with you, don't you think?"

"I can't tell him. Not yet. He's had too many disappointments already." Sheridan sniffled. "Please, Grace. You're the only one I can ask."

"Okay. Just stay calm and keep your feet up. I'll get there as soon as I can."

Disconnecting, Grace immediately tried Ryan's number again, but the call went straight to voice mail. He must still be out of range. She left a quick message explaining about Sheridan and urging Ryan to change his plans and come home.

Then, marching into the living room, she motioned Ms. Purvis over. Angling away from the Burches, she spoke over the yapping puppy and Christina's escalating laughter. "There's been a family emergency. I need to take my sister-in-law to the doctor." She cast an uneasy glance over her shoulder then lowered her voice. "How much longer do you think the Burches will stay?"

"The judge has granted them the entire day, the only stipulation being that they can't remove Christina from the premises." The social worker clasped Grace's arm. "Please, do what you have to do. I'll make certain Christina is safe and well cared for."

Grace felt sick at the idea of leaving while the Burches were still there. She hoped Ryan would get her message and come straight home, because, judging from Christina's excitement level, they were in for a rough evening.

She knew what Ryan would say: *Pray.* If only she had her husband's faith!

I do want to trust You, Lord, she prayed as she drove toward Cross Roads Farm. *I want to trust You for Christina's sake, and for Sheridan's...and most of all, for Ryan and me.*

Twenty minutes later, she parked behind Sheridan's house and rushed inside. She found her sister-in-law reclining on the sofa and knelt beside her. "Oh, honey. How are you feeling?"

"Hurting, but so far it's not as bad as last time." Looking pale and frightened, Sheridan pressed a pillow against her abdomen as she sat up. "Help me to the car?"

Grace gave her a shoulder to lean on. "I still think you should tell Kip."

"I told you why I can't." Sheridan uttered a weak laugh. "Anyway, he and Nathan are over at a farm in Albemarle evaluating a horse someone wants to donate to the program. Hopefully this'll be over one way or another before they get home."

It was the *one way or another* part that worried Grace. She eased Sheridan into the passenger seat then hurried around to the driver's side. Within minutes they were on their way to Sheridan's doctor on the edge of Charlotte.

Spotty cell service, the bane of Ryan's existence.

That, and this blasted custody suit.

Climbing into the pickup after his second appointment of the afternoon, he tried his phone again. It was killing him to know the Burches were at *his house* with *his daughter*, and there wasn't a blasted thing he could do about it.

One bar. One lousy bar. He started driving while holding the phone up to the windshield. A mile down the road he eked out two bars. Maybe enough to—

The voice mail alert chimed, and Grace's number flashed on the screen. Ryan punched the Play button, listening with growing dread as Grace told him about Sheridan. *"I hate leaving Christina like this,"* she said. *"You should be here, Ry. Please come home."*

Ryan thumped the steering wheel, anger igniting in his chest—only he had no idea where to direct his rage. He couldn't be angry with Sheridan for turning to Grace. He couldn't be angry with Grace for leaving to help her sister-in-law.

He *could* be angry with the Burches for putting them all in this situation in the first place.

Or maybe he should just be angry with himself. If only he'd been more accommodating about letting the Burches spend time with Christina, things might never have gone this far.

He whacked the steering wheel again. Aiming the pickup toward Kingsley, he punched Stan Turner's number on his speed dial. When the secretary put the attorney on the line, Ryan said, "Sorry, Stan, but I have to disregard your advice. Grace had an emergency and had to leave, so I'm on my way home."

"Now, take it easy, Ryan. The social worker won't let anything happen."

"You don't understand. When I talked to Grace earlier, it sounded like all the excitement was setting Christina up for a major meltdown." He hauled in an unsteady breath. "I mean it, Stan. I've got a really bad feeling about this visit."

The half hour it took him to get home seemed like a century. He pulled around Ms. Purvis's all-too-familiar green Taurus in his driveway, threw his truck's gearshift into park, and marched across the backyard. Determined to be civil, he purposely slowed his steps and tried to calm his racing thoughts.

Then, as he stepped onto the porch, he heard raised voices and Christina's hysterical shrieks. He burst through the door, nearly tripping over a rodent-size ball of red fur. The animal yelped and skittered under the kitchen table.

"I want my puppy!" Christina cried. "I want my puppy!"

Ryan glanced under the table, where two beady black eyes stared back at him. Turning toward the living room, he found Irene Burch and Nora Purvis surrounding Christina on the sofa, struggling to quiet her.

"What on earth is going on here?" Ryan barely controlled the growl in his voice. Striding forward, he reached past the women and scooped Christina into his arms. He fought to slow his breathing for Christina's sake as he crushed her against his chest and soothed her with firm back rubs. "It's okay, honey. Daddy's here. It's okay."

"I'm so sorry, Mr. O'Keefe." The social worker faced him, hands clasped at her waist. "This is my fault. I should have realized how overexcited Christina was becoming."

"My puppy! My puppy!" Christina sobbed the words into Ryan's shoulder. "Don't let them take my puppy!"

Ryan turned his icy gaze upon Harold Burch. His words hissed through gritted teeth. "You want to explain this?"

Whipping off his glasses, the man pinched the bridge of his nose. "We just thought…"

"More likely you *didn't* think. You intentionally set an innocent little girl up for—"

"Mr. O'Keefe." Ms. Purvis seized Ryan's arm, giving Christina a pointed look.

He drew a long gust of air through his nose and then lowered his voice to a rasping whisper. "We'll have this out later. Right now, I'm taking my daughter to her room to see if I can undo what you've done."

* * *

Grace had lost track of how long she'd been waiting with Sheridan in the exam room. The doctor had performed several tests, including an ultrasound, but hadn't detected a fetal heartbeat.

"That doesn't mean anything," Dr. Purser explained. She offered a reassuring smile. "We're still very early in this pregnancy—"

"So I really am pregnant?" Tears filled Sheridan's eyes.

"Oh, yes." The curly-haired doctor slid reading glasses up her nose and consulted something on her tablet computer. "Tests indicate you're about five weeks along, which would mean a mid-January due date."

"That's wonderful, Sheridan!" Grace pressed her sister-in-law's hand.

"But…the cramps and spotting." Sheridan bit her lip. Her voice shook. "I can't lose this baby, Dr. Purser."

"I agree." The doctor's matter-of-fact tone imbued confidence. "A little spotting is not uncommon at this stage, but with your history we don't want to take any chances." She continued typing on her tablet as she spoke. "I want you on complete bed rest for the time being, which is why I'm checking you into the hospital until we get you stabilized."

Alarm flickered in Sheridan's eyes. "Is that necessary?"

Dr. Purser laughed. "Knowing you, *very* necessary. No way am I allowing you anywhere near horses, dogs, children, or"—she winked—"amorous husbands for at least the next six weeks." As if she could read the doubt in Sheridan's expression, she continued, "I know it's scary, but with early intervention, I think we have a really good chance of helping this little one come to term."

While the doctor left to complete arrangements for admitting Sheridan to the hospital, Grace helped her dress. The hope of seeing her sister-in-law finally become a mother brought a lilt to her voice. "I don't think you have any choice now, Sher. You're going to have to tell Kip."

Sheridan threw her arms around Grace. "I can't believe it. Or maybe I don't want to let myself believe it. What if—"

"None of that!" Wriggling free, Grace gripped Sheridan's shoulders and brushed them gently. "It's going to happen this time, I just know it. You and Kip are going to be parents."

Within the hour, Grace walked beside Sheridan's wheelchair as a hospital volunteer escorted them to a private room. Kip was on his way—and flying higher than the International Space Station, based on what Grace gathered from Sheridan's side of the phone call—but Sheridan had pleaded with Grace to stay until Kip arrived.

He burst through the door a few minutes after five. Tossing his Stetson on the nearest chair, he covered the distance to Sheridan's bed in three long strides. Then inches away he froze, a strange mixture of happiness and hesitation playing havoc with his features. "This is...for real?"

Sheridan nodded and opened her arms to him. When he fell into them, a very uncowboy-like sob exploding from his throat, Grace choked back tears of her own and quietly exited the room.

Please, God, let them keep this baby.

She wasn't sure where it came from, or even if she could trust this strange new feeling, but as she left the hospital to drive back to Kingsley, she had the sweetest, purest sense that this time God would answer their prayers with a *yes*.

Then, as she neared home, her anxiety returned. Her concern for Sheridan had overshadowed any thoughts about how the visit was going with Christina and her grandparents. Could she trust that God had been present there, too?

She turned into the driveway to find only Ryan's pickup and farrier trailer. At least that meant Ms. Purvis and the Burches had gone. But what had they left behind in their wake?

Slipping through the back door, Grace set down her purse, her gaze sweeping the kitchen and living room. She relaxed slightly when she saw Ryan in his easy chair, Christina curled up on his lap. "Is everything okay?"

"It is now." He signaled her over. "Except we've got a new addition to the family."

Grace glanced at the lump of fur snuggled against Christina. "They left the puppy?"

"I told 'em they had to. Want to know how to freak out a four-year-old? Give her a puppy, and then tell her the puppy's gonna be living at *your* house, not hers."

Christina stroked the little dog. "Her name is Gracie."

Grace's eyebrow shot up. She stared at Ryan. "Should I be flattered?"

"Definitely." He grinned at her.

Sinking onto the sofa, Grace reached out to scratch the little dog behind the ears. "I'm really, really sorry I had to leave like that."

"You didn't have a choice. How's Sheridan doing?"

Heart lifting once more, Grace described her afternoon and the hope that with enforced bed rest Sheridan would keep this baby.

"Hallelujah!" Ryan tipped his head back. "That is the best news I've heard all day."

Fatigue catching up with her, Grace burrowed into the sofa cushions. "I'm praying we have some good news of our own soon. I just want this…other stuff…over with."

Later, Grace warmed leftovers for supper while Ryan showered. After they tucked Christina into bed, Ryan led Grace to the sofa and drew her beneath his arm. Peering up at him, she could see the weariness in his eyes and in the slant of his shoulders, and her heart ached for him.

Now that they were alone, she braved the question she'd avoided asking in front of Christina. "How bad was it this afternoon?"

"It was bad." Grimly, Ryan described the scene he'd walked in on. "It took me nearly an hour to calm Christina down." He snorted. "That's how we ended up with a puppy."

"She is kind of cute." Grace glanced at the cardboard box under the kitchen table that served as Gracie's temporary bed. Inside, the pup snuggled with one of Christina's old baby blankets—an arrangement that would probably last only until Gracie was big enough to sleep with Christina. "Do you think Ms. Purvis's report will go in our favor?"

Ryan shrugged. "Either the Burches will come across as completely clueless about how to care for an Aspie kid, or I'll look like a monster for snapping at them like I did."

"They deserved it. And they *are* clueless." Grace cuddled closer, snaking an arm around Ryan's torso. She never knew loving someone this much could feel so wonderful... so right.

A quiver began deep in her abdomen, a longing unlike anything she'd ever experienced. Maybe it was the aftermath of what they'd each gone through today, or maybe it was being reminded once more of the deep, lasting love between Kip and Sheridan. Grace only knew that she couldn't lose her own chance at love.

She couldn't lose Ryan.

Trust your heart.

Tonight, finally, it told her she was ready...ready to love her husband with everything she could offer.

She lifted her hand to his cheek, feeling the stubble of his late-day beard, breathing in the working-man scent of soap and a clean, cottony T-shirt. Gazing deep into his eyes, hoping her meaning would be crystal-clear, she murmured, "It's been a long day, honey. Let's go to bed."

* * *

Ryan had never felt so content, so utterly replete with happiness. Grace's invitation Thursday night was an answered prayer, and the three days since had proved this marriage to be everything he'd ever hoped for. Grace was a caring and supportive wife, a gentle and patient mother, a warm and passionate lover. If there really was such a thing as a soul mate, Ryan had found her.

Even so, as he started the coffee brewing Monday morning, he couldn't shake the underlying fear that all this could be taken away from him in an instant. Not Grace—no, he knew she'd stand by him, whatever the future held. But if that future didn't include his daughter—*their* daughter—

His body convulsed with a physical pain. Both hands braced on the counter, he lowered his head. *God, please...*

Grace stroked his back, her touch firm and reassuring. "It'll be okay. I know it will."

He swiveled to face her. Drawing her close, he nestled his chin in the softness of her hair. "Without you, this would be so much harder. The best decision I ever made was asking you to be my wife."

"The best decision *I* ever made was saying yes—the first time, and then..." She shivered with a contented sigh and burrowed deeper into his embrace.

He'd give anything if she didn't have to drive into Charlotte today for the first day of summer classes. And if Christina and her puppy would only sleep another hour or so...

"Daddy." A tug on his jeans put an end to his daydreams. "Gracie wants breakfast, and so do I."

"Good morning to you, too, sleepyhead." With a reluctant groan, Ryan released his wife and reached down to tousle Christina's curls. The frisky pup squirmed in her arms, pink tongue darting faster than hummingbird wings.

"You get the puppy chow; I'll get the people chow."

Shooting Ryan a meaningful smile, Grace stepped toward the fridge. "I've got to get a move on or I'll be late for class."

As soon as they finished breakfast, Grace gathered up her purse and book satchel. Ryan walked her to the door and made sure his good-bye kiss expressed exactly how much he would miss her. "Drive safe. I love you, Mrs. O'Keefe."

"Have I mentioned lately how much I like the sound of that?" Grinning, she flicked the end of his nose. "I love you, too, Mr. O'Keefe." Starting out the door, she turned with a chiding glance. "Chin up, okay? No moping around and letting worry get the best of you. God's in control."

Hearing her say that as if she believed it encouraged Ryan like nothing else. While Grace battled her doubts, Ryan had fought hard to be the strong one, to convince her God was faithful. Now she'd turned the tables on him, and it felt good to rest in someone else's strength for a while.

Yes, indeed, marrying Grace was the smartest thing he'd ever done.

After pouring another mug of coffee, Ryan settled at the kitchen table with Christina to work on her reading and numbers skills. Anything he could relate to horses and puppies, she picked up rapidly.

As he started Christina on a counting workbook page, the doorbell rang—a sound he'd come to dread these past few weeks. Muscles tensing, he pushed up from the table. "Keep working, sugarplum. I'll be right back."

When he peered through the peephole and saw the Burches, his gut clenched. Primed to bodily escort Christina's grandparents off his property, he yanked open the door. "What are you doing here? Don't tell me you got another court order."

Harold Burch flattened his lips. "That isn't why we came."

Aware of his daughter only a few feet away, Ryan stepped onto the porch and pulled the door shut. "Then what do you want? And make it quick, because last time you were here, you bled me dry of every last ounce of patience."

"We know." Mrs. Burch sniffled. She clutched her purse at her waist. "We're so sorry, Ryan."

The retort waiting on Ryan's lips melted away. He blinked slowly, not sure he'd heard right.

Mr. Burch seemed to look everywhere but at Ryan. Finally he lowered his head and sighed. "We've made mistakes. Lots of mistakes. We came to tell you in person that we're dropping the custody suit."

The words slammed through Ryan like a jolt of electricity. He grabbed the porch rail before his knees gave way. "You…you're serious?"

"We've done a lot of thinking since last Thursday." Mr. Burch rested his arm around his wife's shoulders. "Seeing Christina so upset, realizing it was our fault… We love her dearly, but we've had to face the fact that we are not equipped, emotionally or physically, to give her the kind of parenting she needs."

"You're a good father, Ryan." Mrs. Burch dabbed her eyes. "And your new wife is a good mother to Christina. We could tell how much she loves her."

"Thank you." The words seared Ryan's throat. His chest ached with relief and gratitude. "I'm sorry, too, for how I've resisted letting Christina visit. I promise that'll change."

Standing taller, Mr. Burch said, "I want you to know Irene and I are joining an Asperger support group in Shelby. We're going to learn all we can about Christina's…differentness…so we'll be better able to help." His jaw muscles bunched. "If you'll allow us, that is."

Ryan swiped at his brimming eyes. "That'd be great."

The door opened, and Ryan pivoted to see Christina

standing on the sill. She skewed her lips and counted on her fingers. "I wrote down four ducks, three cows, seven cats, nine elephants, and two penguins. Now I want some cookies."

Laughing out loud, Ryan scooped her into his arms and hugged her as if he could never let her go.

Arriving home from class shortly after noon, Grace jammed on the brakes in a panic when she recognized the Burches' silver sedan in the driveway. "Dear God, please, no..."

She sat in the car for a full two minutes while trying to work up the courage to go inside. Would this mean the end of all their hopes? Would God really allow the Burches to take Christina?

Be strong and take heart, all you who hope in the Lord.

The last verse of Psalm 31, Pastor Wolfe's sermon theme yesterday, had been playing through her thoughts all morning. She would not lose hope, no matter what she found when she walked through the back door. She and Ryan would face it together and trust God to see them through.

Still, her hand shook as she turned the knob. She inched the door open and edged inside.

"Hey, hon, just in time." Looking slightly dazed, Ryan carried a skillet of grilled cheese sandwiches to the table, where Christina and the Burches sat waiting. Christina seemed calm and happy. The Burches looked...strangely subdued.

Grace swallowed. "What's going on here?"

Ryan set the skillet in the center of the table. "Help yourselves. I'll be right back." He hooked his arm around Grace and ushered her out to the porch. Gripping her by the shoulders, he stared deep into her eyes, a huge grin lighting his face. "It's over, Grace. It's over!"

"Over." She rolled the word around in her brain. "You mean—"

"They dropped the suit. We're keeping Christina!"

"Oh, Ryan!" Happiness exploded in her chest like a hundred Roman candles going off at once. She threw her arms around her husband and squeezed until neither of them could catch a breath. Eventually she'd make him tell her everything, help her understand exactly how this came about.

But for now all she wanted was to celebrate with the man she adored and praise the God who, even when she refused to believe, never let them give up hope.

Epilogue

Two years later

Ryan stooped to snag another root beer from the cooler then plopped into the porch swing next to Kip. "So, why is it exactly they don't let guys attend these things?"

Kip looked at him like he was crazy and gulped another swig of cola.

"Believe me, we would be way out of our comfort zone in there." Nathan scooped cheese dip onto a tortilla chip, holding it just out of twenty-month-old Rosalinda's reach. "I mean, do you *really* want to try diapering a baby-doll with a blindfold over your eyes?"

Kip rolled his eyes as he rose to lasso his little son, who'd raced his plastic horses too close to the porch steps. "And don't even get me started on guessing your pregnant wife's stomach measurement. You really want to start World War III?"

"Yeah, but you guys have all been through this before. This is a first for Grace and me. I hate missing a minute of it."

The back door opened, and three very pregnant women strolled out. Nathan glanced up and grabbed Filipa's hand. "Is the shower over already?"

"Nope, just checking on the menfolk." Filipa lifted Rosalinda and nuzzled her cheek. "Is your daddy behaving, *mija*?"

Sheridan chuckled as little Kenneth, her towheaded one-year-old, toddled over to show her his horses. "Like father, like son." She tucked her arm around Kip's waist and grinned up at him. "Are you ready to do this again so soon?"

Clasping her by the nape, he planted a kiss on her smiling lips. "You bet. 'Cause I can't wait to get busy on number three."

Grace scooted in next to Ryan on the swing, one hand pressing hard against the upper right side of her abdomen. "We're either having a soccer player or a karate champ."

"Either one's fine with me." Ryan caressed the spot on Grace's tummy where it appeared a tiny foot was moving.

She gasped at another kick. "Easy there, little one." Catching her breath, she glanced around and asked, "Where's Christina?"

"The granddads took her for a walk with the dogs—or more likely the dogs are walking them." Ryan chuckled at the thought of his little Christina hand in hand with big Tom Jacobs and Manuelo Beltran, Filipa's dad, all of them getting dragged along the lane by a lumbering Great Dane and a frisky Pomeranian.

The back door opened again, and Linda Jacobs peeked out. "Hey, gals, you still have gifts to open."

Ryan rose with Grace then turned a withering look upon

Kip and Nathan. "You guys can stay out here if you want. I'm joining the party."

Eyes lighting with surprise, Grace smiled up at him. "I hoped you'd say that."

He paused on the threshold to sear her lips with a long, lazy kiss and gazed into eyes so brimming with love that they made his chest hurt. "Have I told you lately that I'm crazy about you, Mrs. O'Keefe?"

"Not often enough, Mr. O'Keefe. Not often enough."

* * * * *

HEARTSONG

PRESENTS

Look out for 4 new
Heartsong Presents books next month!

**Every month 4 inspiring faith-filled
romances will be available in stores.**

These contemporary and historical Christian
romances emphasize God's role in every
relationship and reinforce the importance of
faith, hope and love.

REQUEST YOUR FREE BOOKS!

2 FREE CHRISTIAN NOVELS
PLUS 2
FREE
MYSTERY GIFTS

H E A R T S O N G
P R E S E N T S

REQUEST YOUR FREE BOOKS!

2 FREE INSPIRATIONAL NOVELS
PLUS 2
FREE
MYSTERY GIFTS

Love Inspired

LIDIR13

ReaderService.com

Manage your account online!

- Review your order history
- Manage your payments
- Update your address

We've designed the Harlequin® Reader Service website just for you.

Enjoy all the features!

- Reader excerpts from any series
- Respond to mailings and special monthly offers
- Discover new series available to you
- Browse the Bonus Bucks catalog
- Share your feedback

Visit us at:
ReaderService.com

RS13

Sweetheart Bride

by *New York Times* bestselling author

Lenora Worth

Restoring not just a house but a heart, as well

When architect Nick Santiago recruits Brenna Blanchard to help restore a beautiful old mansion, it's just the distraction she needs from her recent broken wedding engagement—and growing close to handsome Nick is an unexpected bonus. Except, Nick is all business. Can Brenna help him arrange his priorities—with love as number one?

Available February 2013!

www.LoveInspiredBooks.com